The drumming of the shower quit, and with it, Ty's time ran out.

No doubt in another life he'd do whatever it took to make Mia a permanent fixture in his life and his bed.

Unfortunately, he was stuck in this life. And Mia Serrat was unreachable. Untouchable, at least by him.

She almost ran into him before she saw him in the doorway. They stood toe-to-toe, so close he could feel the heat rising from her skin. So close he could see the same heat in her eyes. Eyes that were locked on him.

"I want to believe you," he finally said.

"Shh," she said, and put a finger to his lips. "Don't."

Her finger was rose-petal soft on his mouth, and he wanted to pull it inside, devour it, taste it. Instead, he shifted just enough to brush the pad a little harder. A whisper of a kiss...

Dear Reader,

Writing a book is often a gradual process of building a world, characters and a plot one decision at a time, agonizing over each small choice for a period of days, weeks and months. Once in a while, though, an author is lucky enough to be struck by a novel idea fully formed. The characters, the plot, the twists, the conflict flood her mind in a single bombardment of images and voices. The author becomes merely a scribe, taking down what has been given to her. *A Doctor's Watch* is one such story, and I'm very pleased to bring it to you with the help of Silhouette Romantic Suspense.

Mia Serrat is a strong woman, but she's been through some really tough times. For the sake of her young son, she fought to regain her health after a debilitating bout with depression and she succeeded. Or so she thinks.

Dr. Ty Hanson is the one man who can help her convince everyone that she's not crazy, but his own history and his feelings for Mia complicate his professional judgment.

I hope you enjoy their story.

Vickie Taylor

VICKIE TAYLOR

A Doctor's Watch

Silhouette®

Romantic
SUSPENSE

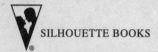

SILHOUETTE BOOKS

ISBN-13: 978-0-373-27664-6

A DOCTOR'S WATCH

Visit Silhouette Books at www.eHarlequin.com

Printed in U.S.A.

Books by Vickie Taylor

VICKIE TAYLOR

is the bestselling author of more than a dozen romantic-suspense and paranormal romance novels. She is a four-time finalist for a Romance Writers of America RITA® Award and is the winner of a Daphne du Maurier Award of Excellence in mystery/suspense fiction. When not writing or reading, Vickie spends her time riding horses, training search-and-rescue dogs and volunteering for her local humane society. For up-to-date news and information, visit Vickie at www.VickieTaylor.com.

Many, many thanks to my editor, Ann Leslie Tuttle. You set me on this crazy road of publication, and you've stuck with me through the good times and the bad. Without you, this book and many others would never have seen the light of day.

Chapter 1

Five more good days. A quick tally of all the other groups of five ticks in her diary added up to three hundred and ten. Three hundred and ten good days. Days without shadows. Days without darkness lurking inside her.

Days without depression.

Mia Serrat smiled. Despite the stark white winter landscape outside her window, she felt as bright as the California sun she'd been imagining. As fresh as the sea air. Soon she would go home to California for real, away from the cold and snow of Massachusetts.

Now all she had to do was tell Nana.

A knot of apprehension coiled in her belly. She'd

already waited too long to talk to her mother-in-law, but she wouldn't wait any longer. Today was the day—as soon as she'd had her morning run.

Heading downstairs, she buoyed herself by humming a pop tune about soaking up the sun.

"You could take a day off, you know," Nana called from the kitchen as Mia bounced into the foyer, reaching for her scarf from the coat tree by the door. "It's freezing outside."

Undaunted, Mia wrapped the scarf around her neck and grabbed her gloves. Not even Nana's motherly nagging, or the difficult conversation ahead between them, could keep her from enjoying the start of a new day. Already her blood was flowing faster, her breath coming deeper in anticipation of her daily workout. "I dressed warmly."

"It's icy."

"I'll be careful." She followed the scent of fresh-baked cinnamon rolls toward the kitchen, where she would undoubtedly find her eight-year-old son with a full stomach and an icing mustache. "Smells like you're spoiling Todd again."

"Won't hurt the boy to be fussed over now and then."

Mia gave Nana a hug in the kitchen doorway to let her know how much she appreciated everything the older woman did for them. "No, I suppose it won't."

She caught Todd's eye over the rim of his milk glass. "Hey, tigerbear."

He thunked down his glass and groaned. "Mo-om."

"Oh, sorry. I mean *Sir* Samuel Todd Serrat." He

was so sensitive to anything remotely childish these days. Including pet names.

"Todd would do."

"Gotcha."

His face brightened as he nodded toward the platter in the center of the table. "I saved ya the last roll."

"Thanks, but I'll catch a yogurt after my run."

"Yogurt? Bleck!" He grabbed the lone sticky bun and grinned.

She ruffled his hair. "I'm getting in shape. It's called exercise. You should try it sometime instead of sitting in front of your computer all the time playing video games."

The cinnamon roll puffed out his cheeks like a chipmunk's when he smiled. "I get plenty of exercise. Just this morning I fought off a squad of Ninja hit men, slayed two dragons and saved the world from an alien invasion."

Even Nana laughed at that.

"Have you decided what you want for Christmas, mighty warrior?" Mia asked, and then held up her hand. "Besides computer games?"

"Christmas?" Nana asked, winking as her gaze swiveled from Mia to Todd. "Is it that time of year already?"

But Todd wasn't biting on her feigned indifference to childhood's mega holiday of holidays. Still, his bright eyes darkened.

"You don't gotta get me nothing."

"Of course we do." Mia's heart fluttered around in her chest like a tiny trapped bird. "It's Christmas!"

"Christmas is for kids." His shoulders stiffened.

"I hate to break it to you, but eight years old still qualifies as a kid in my book."

"I said I don't want nothing, all right." Todd dropped the cinnamon roll on his plate, scraped his chair back and made a grab for his books as he stood.

Her hands balled on her hips. Todd had always loved Christmas. "No, it is not all right." She scooted in front of him before he could make a break for the back door.

Lowering her arms, she took a deep breath and waited. After several long seconds, Todd slowly raised his head and looked up at her through the sheaf of dusty-blond lashes he'd inherited from his daddy.

Suddenly, Mia could have sworn she was looking into the eyes of an eighty-year-old man in her son's body. His sad gaze wrapped around her heart and squeezed.

She'd done this. She'd put the darkness in her child's eyes. She knew the exact day, the exact time she'd done it.

The week before Christmas two years ago, when she'd tried to kill herself.

Mia swallowed the lump in her throat. She'd put the darkness in Todd, the fear, and she would take it away, she vowed. No matter how many years, how many Christmases it took.

"You don't gotta get me nothing," he mumbled. "Don't worry about it. Christmas is dumb anyway."

Straightening up, she took a deep breath and smiled brightly on the outside even as she died a little more inside at his words.

Don't worry about it.

It pained her, knowing her family still thought her so fragile.

"Try to think of a present that involves something we could do together, okay?" she said. "Like jigsaw puzzles or something." Something that would reassure him that she wasn't going anywhere. She forced a placid smile to her face. "And you'd better come up with something soon, or you might just get socks and underwear."

Todd's frail shoulders relaxed a bit. "Eww…"

Mia kissed his wrinkled nose, then pulled his coat off the hook by the back door and held it out to him. "You'd better get going. The bus will be here any minute. Be good today."

With the heavy sigh of a child faced with seven hours of sitting still and keeping quiet—and a mother he didn't quite trust to be here when he got home—Todd pulled on his coat.

Nana tucked his scarf in around his neck and smooched him and threw an air kiss as he tromped out the door. "Love you."

"Love you, too." He waved without looking back.

Inside, apprehension flipped Mia's stomach. The house was quiet. She'd barely navigated her way through one difficult conversation, and now she was more determined than ever to have another one, this time with Nana. It was time to tell Nana she was leaving, the sooner the better. If nothing else, Todd's reaction to Christmas had reinforced how badly she needed some time alone with her son. Time to rebuild his trust in her.

First, she needed tea. She heated water in the microwave, then dunked a bag of her favorite green tea in the mug while Nana busied herself with the dishes in the sink.

"I called the property management company," Mia said. "The one who's been looking after the house in Malibu." She tried for calm, confident strength in her voice, but couldn't help but notice the little squeak at the end of the sentence. "She said they could have the utilities turned on and everything cleaned and opened up right after the first of the year."

Nana's shoulders stiffened. Dishes clattered. "So soon?"

"School starts on the fifth of January."

Nana turned, the dishcloth twisted in her hands. "Put him in a new class in the middle of the year? Is that wise after all he's been through?"

Another pang of guilt stabbed through her.

"I talked to the counselor at the elementary. She said it's actually easier for kids to transition during the school year. They have a chance to make new friends right away instead of sitting home alone during the summer, waiting for a new term."

Nana leaned heavily on the counter behind her. "Are you sure you're ready? What if you…?"

Mia pulled her shoulders back. Now was not the time to question herself. "You know you can come visit us anytime, Nana."

"It just wouldn't be the same as having you here, under my roof." Her eyes brimmed. "And besides, I have Citria and Karl here."

Mia hated making Nana choose between her grandson and her daughter and brother. Nana's roots were here. Still…

"You'd love California. It's warm and sunny all the time. Your arthritis—"

"I couldn't. I—I've lived all my life in Eternal."

"Then we'll come visit you, in the summer when Todd is out of school."

Nana turned back to the sink and attacked the dishes with a vengeance that might leave the household short a few china plates if she didn't ease up. "You don't have to decide today. We've still got three weeks before Christmas."

Mia's heart hurt, but she lifted her chin. "Yes, we've got time." Time, she hoped, for Nana to accept the inevitable, and for Mia to accept that she had no choice but to break her mother-in-law's heart.

She needed to take her life back—for all their sakes. She'd worked hard to get healthy again. She needed her independence.

"I thought you were going for a run," Nana said, her jaw stiff. "You're all dressed for it."

Understanding Nana's veiled request for some time alone, Mia downed the last of her tea and stood. At the back door, she doubled over to stretch her calves, then lifted each foot behind her in turn and pulled, loosening her hamstrings. "I'll see you in an hour."

Before she could leave, Nana snugged up the crimson scarf around Mia's neck, tucking the ends beneath her collar just as she had for Todd. The wool would be scratchy, Mia thought, especially when she started to sweat, but she accepted the coddling without comment. Nana was just looking out for her. Lord knew there'd been a time when she'd needed it.

She set off across the yard, toward the bike trail to Shilling's Bluff, at an easy pace, giving her muscles time to warm. Her thoughts drifted at random. Running put her in an almost meditative state, and soon she found herself pondering Todd's Christmas gift again.

She had a feeling he wanted something special, but hadn't worked up the gumption to tell her yet. She would have to talk to Nana later and see if she knew what it was. Otherwise, she might make a critical holiday faux pas, and she so wanted Todd to be happy this year. He deserved it.

Heart pumping harder now, she turned off the bike path onto the hiking trail up the bluff. Her breath clouded in front of her face. The snow was deeper here. It drifted in piles against rocks and clung to the boughs of the evergreens crowded on the side of the trail opposite the cliff.

As she climbed higher, the town emerged in the valley below, white tufts of snow scalloping the eaves of the buildings along Main Street and dusting the sidewalks.

Todd said that after a snowfall, Eternal looked like the village in one of those snow globes kids played with, just waiting to be shaken. On mornings like this, she agreed with him.

He was such a smart kid, and thoughtful, too. She wished his father could have seen how he'd grown up. He would be so proud.

Mia's ankle turned on the steep slope. She slipped and stumbled, but caught her balance before losing her footing altogether. Her heart stuttered as she tried to recapture her rhythm. Her arms swung jerkily and her feet landed unevenly.

It annoyed her that a simple stray thought of her husband, Todd's father, Sam Serrat, was enough to make the dark cloud that was never far behind her seem to loom directly overhead. She quickened her pace to escape it.

Depression couldn't be outrun, she knew, no matter how long or how hard she tried. But she could stay one step ahead of it. As long as the darkness was behind her, and not inside, she would be okay.

Three hundred and ten days, she reminded herself. She'd worked hard to get her life back, and she'd succeeded. She wouldn't lose herself again. She wouldn't lose Todd.

Cautiously, she let herself think about her husband again. The way his sandy hair fell over his eyes when he laughed. The sense of humor and compassion he'd passed to his son, even though he was gone before Todd ever really knew him. The way he made love to her so slowly, so gently, she thought it might last forever.

Only, nothing lasted forever. She'd learned that the hard way.

Tears filled her eyes, but they didn't spill over. Time diminished the pain his memory caused. Each day she hurt a little less when she thought of Sam.

Todd was what kept her going now. He was the reason she'd worked so hard these last two years to take her life back from depression.

Muscles quivering with exertion, she plunged up the last few feet to the top of the bluff and stood with her hands on her hips, blowing hard. Forty feet below her, a winding road cut through the granite rise that made Shillings Bluff. Right on time, the yellow school bus lumbered around the turn.

Mia started jogging again, slowly, letting the bus catch her. She sped up as it pulled even, feigned a hard run as it overtook her.

Todd sat in the backseat, as he always did, face plastered against the rear window as he watched her. He waved and encouraged her on. She ran faster, pretending to race the bus, pretending to go all out. It was their game. Their ritual.

With Todd bouncing in his seat, she lowered her head. Kicked harder. Stole a glance at her son, and his sweet face took her breath away as the bus pulled ahead and around a bend. She—

Something solid—a hand—thunked between Mia's shoulder blades. She tried to turn to see who had hit her from behind, but the blow had thrown her off balance. Her sneaker skidded on a patch of ice. Her other toe caught on a rock. She flailed.

Mia tried to throw herself back onto the path. Away from the granite slope. She failed. She fell.

And she screamed, but no one heard. Or if they did, they didn't care.

Chapter 2

Crap, crap, crap.

Ty Hansen cursed all the way to his car, but the sound was lost in the swoosh of the north wind that sailed right through his leather bomber jacket and chilled him to the bone. Snow-laden clouds hung low overhead, ready to dump their payload. Already the first tiny flakes stung his face like icy needles. He shoved his hands in his pockets, hunched his shoulders against the miserable weather.

Talk about tap dancing in minefields.

Why the hell did he have to be the one to draw the Kaiser's niece as a patient?

"The Kaiser," as Karl Serrat was called by the staff when he was out of hearing range, oversaw all the residents in the psychiatric specialty program at the Massachusetts Hospital of Mental Health. They all considered him a taskmaster, but he seemed to ride Ty particularly hard. He also held Ty's entire future—his completion of the residency program required before taking the exams from the American Board of Medical Specialties to become a licensed psychiatrist—in his twisted grasp.

The man was just looking for an excuse to kick him out. Karl Serrat had been on Ty's back since their first meeting.

With the snow, the drive to Eternal took an hour and a half. Stomping his boots and shrugging out of his jacket at the ER nurses' station, he asked the large-boned African-American woman behind the desk for the psych consult file and plowed down the hallway, reading the patient history as he walked.

He tapped twice with his knuckle on the door to evaluation room 5, counted to three to give her a few seconds to pull herself together, then took a deep breath and poked his head in. "Ms. Serrat, may I come in?"

The hell with Karl Serrat. He had a job to do and it didn't matter if the woman waiting for him was Serrat's niece or Mona Lisa. She was a patient, and he would do his best by her, consequences be damned.

Fixing that thought firmly in his mind, he pasted on a smile and said "Hi, I'm Dr.—"

The woman who turned to look at him from her place by the window nearly made him forget his own name. It wasn't her beauty so much that stymied him, though she had that, as her intensity.

She stood as far away from the door as she could get. If she hadn't been holding a disposable cup, he was sure her arms would have been folded tightly over her chest, fingers fisted. Her tousled mahogany hair was thrown back over her shoulders and her full mouth pursed slightly. Her eyes, as lush, green and mysterious as a tropical rain forest, glinted with tightly controlled anger.

Obviously she'd figured out he wasn't here to give a second opinion on her bumps and bruises. Yet, instead of pouting about a psychological evaluation, or retreating inside herself, there was a challenge in her eyes.

The woman wasn't just all good looks. She had moxie.

"Dr.—?" she asked, hooking one eyebrow.

"Hansen. Ms. uh—" He cleared his throat. "Serrat."

She studied him critically. "My uncle sent you, I assume."

"Uh, yeah." *Brilliant. Very eloquent.*

Sighing in resignation, she hopped up on the edge of the examination table. "Well, let's get this over with. I have a son to get home to." Her feet dangled off the floor, exposing the delicate bare ankles at the ends of two very long legs.

"Sure. Uh, yeah."

Heaven help him.

Mia had prepared herself to do battle with some pasty-skinned, condescending head-shrinker who had his name sewn over the breast pocket of his lab coat and who spoke through his nasal passages. She was ready, or she thought she was.

Never in her wildest dreams had she imagined they'd send someone like young Dr. Handsome, here, to check up on her. One look at him, and her game plan fell apart with an audible crash.

He was tall and tanned and lean, but with enough bulk under his blue denim button-down dress shirt to hint at a fit body. His hair was conservatively cut, but just enough overdue for a trim that the light brown ends curled over his collar. A few flakes of snow still clung in the cowlick over his left temple.

The cold had left ruddy spots on his cheeks, and the beginnings of a slight shadow darkened his jaw, but not grimly. The stubble, combined with brilliant hazel eyes, a lazy smile that only reached one side of his mouth and the battered leather jacket slung over his shoulder gave him a slightly harried, sleepy, sexy look.

She wasn't ready for him at all.

She wondered if he knew exactly how disarming that lopsided grin of his could be. She wondered whether it was genuine or part of his psychotherapy-babble bag of tricks.

"Ms. Serrat?" He lifted his eyebrows in question.

Polite, too, still waiting for her to invite him in. Not a common trait in doctors, in her experience.

Despite his charm and his manners, she jutted her chin when she nodded, reminding herself he was the man standing between her and Todd. She needed to get home to her son, preferably before school let out for the day. She didn't want him to know anything about this little incident.

He shouldered his way through the door and eased across the room, stopping about three feet away and extending his hand. Tricky, he was. Making her go to him. A subtle but effective shifting of power in the room.

On another day, she would have refused to play his mind games. But today, she decided an antisocial display would not further her cause.

Hopping off the exam table and stepping forward, she accepted his hand. His knuckles were scraped and swollen as though he'd been in a fight, she noticed. Young Dr. Handsome was one surprise after another.

Before she thought better of herself, she swept her thumb over the abrasions. "Rough day at the office, Doc?"

He looked puzzled for a second, then glanced down and extricated his hand from hers. "Just a little difference of opinion."

It was her turn to look puzzled, but she didn't ask for an explanation, nor did he offer one. It was best they get down to business, anyway.

"I'm sorry you had to wait so long," he said, throwing his jacket across the foot of the bed. "I'd have been here an hour ago, but the weather's taking a turn for the worse and the roads are getting nasty."

An hour. What was one hour? she wondered.

An eternity to an eight-year-old boy. A boy waiting for his mother.

"Why don't we get this over with so you can get back on the road to wherever home is, then?"

"Sounds like a plan." He rubbed his hands together to warm them, looking her up and down.

Her spine tingled as if he'd run his fingers up her back. The look hadn't been sexual at all—it was definitely a doctor's appraising gaze.

Still, she had felt it.

As if he'd felt it, too, he took a step back.

Even fully clothed and with four feet of distance between them, she felt naked. Bare to the soul. Unable to resist any longer, she set her tea down and crossed her arms over the buttercup-yellow flannel pajama top Nana had brought for her.

She wished Nana had brought clothes, instead.

"How are you feeling?" he asked.

"Fine," she lied. Her hip hurt like hell. "The doctor gave me a clean bill of health."

"Good. Do you know why I'm here?"

Her lips pressed together in a bleak smile. "You're a psychologist."

"Psychiatrist, actually. You know what happens next?"

She nodded and sat on the edge of the bed, her legs hanging over the side. She'd been through this before. At least he wasn't patronizing her.

He asked a battery of questions. Her name. The

date. The name of the current president. The immediate former president. Who's buried in Grant's tomb?

She looked up at him quizzically. "Grant?"

He grinned. "Just seeing if you were paying attention. Thought I had you there."

"My son loves riddles. I hear that one, or some variation on it, at least once a week."

"What happened this morning?" Dr. Handsome asked. His gaze followed her as she hopped off the bed and paced, limping. She didn't want to do this, but he wasn't going to let her go home to Todd until she did.

"Why don't you just come right out and ask me?" she said, hating the impatience in her voice.

"Ask you what?"

"If I tried to kill myself again."

"Did you try to kill yourself again?" he said without missing a beat.

"No."

"But you have tried before."

Statement, not question. No sense denying it, she thought. The facts would be in her medical record.

"A long time ago," she said flatly.

"After you lost your husband?"

"And my sister six months before that, and my parents a year before that." Her heart constricted painfully at the memory. Memories.

A moment of silence passed. "That's a lot to go through in eighteen months."

"Too much." She turned to him, her lips pressed in a grim line. "Or so I thought at the time."

His smile was gone, and the look that had replaced it brought a lump to her throat. His face glowed with a warm, quiet concern.

Compassion.

"But not anymore?" he asked.

She took a deep breath, raw at having to expose herself like this to a stranger. Most people had a right to privacy. To dignity. Not so the mentally ill, or those suspected of mental illness. They were expected to drag their deepest fears, their most personal vulnerabilities out for inspection by anyone with the right abbreviations or acronyms behind their names.

She considered lying, knew it would only delay the inevitable. He would pick at her until he got the truth.

Looking down, she saw her hands were trembling and clasped them together to hide the weakness. "I spent eight months in the hospital learning to deal with my grief. I clawed my way back to normalcy day by day. Sometimes minute by minute or second by second, but I made it." She threw her chin in the air. "My doctor there had me keep a journal. I still do it. I record my good days and bad days and why each was the way it was. As of this morning, I'd had three hundred and ten consecutive good days. Three hundred and ten."

When she dropped her gaze again, she realized she'd fisted her hands so tightly her knuckles had gone white.

Dr. Hansen gave her a few seconds to collect herself, then asked gently, "What happened this morning?"

She hesitated. "I fell."

He checked the file, then said in that same placid, calming tone, "You told the police you were pushed."

"I was confused. I hit my head." She touched the knot on her temple as if to prove it. Damn it, she shouldn't have to prove anything to him.

But she did, if she wanted to go home, and she did want to go home, even if it meant lying. She'd told the police and the first doctor who had examined her that she'd been pushed into the road.

It hadn't gone over well.

She ducked her chin. She would not give him reason to call her paranoid. "Maybe some snow slid off the trees and hit me in the back. The sun was warming things up pretty good."

She lifted her head. "Or maybe I just stumbled. That's how I ended up in the road." Desperately, she tried to give him a reassuring grin. It wobbled and she gave up. "I did not throw myself over a cliff on purpose."

To her surprise, he smiled back. "Good."

She rolled her shoulder, feeling the tension easing out. He believed her. Didn't he?

He made a few notes on her file and then raised his head. "What were you thinking about before you fell?"

"Todd's Christmas present. My son, he's eight. I was deciding what to get him."

He made a sympathetic noise. "Tough age to buy for. Young enough he still wants all the good kids' toys, but too old to admit it."

"Exactly." She couldn't believe he understood. Maybe there was more to him than a pretty face. "You have kids?"

"No, but I was one once. And I know how little boys' minds work. I am male."

Surprising herself, she swept her eyes from his broad shoulders to his lean waist, long legs and back up again.

Definitely male.

It had been a long time since she'd noticed that about anyone.

"So what did you decide on?" He grinned at her. She couldn't decide if he knew exactly what she'd been thinking or if he was really as innocently naive as he seemed.

"I didn't," she explained, heat rising to her cheeks. Focus. She needed to focus on the conversation. She had no business noticing anything about this man. He was a doctor. The doctor who held the power to declare her sane or crazy. "I was wishing my husband were there. He would know what to get."

"How did it make you feel that he wasn't there?"

She snorted, suddenly disappointed in Dr. Handsome. "Oh, please. Not the 'how did it make you feel' question. How do you think it made me feel?"

"Sad? Lonely?"

She wrinkled her nose. "Have you ever been married?"

"No."

"Maybe if you had, you'd have some inkling of what it means to be twenty-five years old, with a four-year-old baby and to lose all the family you have, not to mention the man you love, the only man you've ever been with, without warning. Until then, don't pretend to understand what I do or don't feel about my dead husband."

He stilled the pencil he'd been twirling between his fingers and looked her right in the eye. "Well said, and with lots of feeling. You're very good. How many doctors have you used that shtick on?"

The accusation took her aback. Until she recognized it as the truth. "A few."

"Did it work?"

"More times than not."

He strolled toward her, his tongue in his cheek. "Then you've been seeing the wrong doctors."

He locked his golden gaze on hers and she couldn't look away.

"Let's try this again," he said, towering over her. "How were you feeling just before you fell?"

The irrational urge to run swept over her. He was too close. Physically and emotionally. He smelled like Polo cologne.

And tasted like fear. Her fear.

She was not crazy. She wouldn't let anyone say she was.

"If you want me to say I was depressed, you can go to hell," she said.

"Been there. Didn't care for it." His face remained impassive, but his eyes changed. Cool intellect gave way to a dark, hot fury that burned somewhere deep inside him. The kind of fury only someone who has suffered could feel.

"Me neither," she said. "Depression was my hell. I almost had to die to do it, but I escaped. I won't ever go back."

He looked away as if he suddenly found their linked gazes too intimate. "You're one of the lucky ones, then."

"I am." She touched the scars on his right forearm and he flinched as though she'd burned him. "What about you?"

"I'm working on it." He raised his head, cupped her chin and looked into her eyes again, his own fires now banked. "I—" His fingers tightened on her face. "Damn."

"What?"

"Did the ER doctor give you something when he treated you? Pain medication? A sedative?"

"No."

"Your pupils are big as dinner plates." He let her go and cursed again. "I can't sign off on the evaluation if you're medicated."

She followed him when he turned his back and marched away. "I don't need to be evaluated. I just need to go home. To my son. Please."

He groaned like a man in pain. "I can't. I have to talk to you when your head is clear. I can't afford to mess this up. Director Serrat—"

"Uncle Karl?"

He stiffened, and she knew she'd made a mistake mentioning her uncle. His boss.

He picked up his jacket and shrugged into it without turning. "I'll come back to finish the evaluation tomorrow."

"Let me go home and I'll come to you in Belier in the morning."

He shook his head. "I'm sorry. I just can't risk it."

Understanding exploded with a burst of bitterness on her tongue. "Worried about my life or your career?"

"Neither," he said stiffly. "You have a son."

Rage rose to the surface. "I would never hurt my son. Never!"

"I'll talk to you tomorrow." He headed toward the door, but stopped just inside, shoulders stiff.

"Wait. Please!" Desperation propelled her across the room after him. She stopped just short of touching him, her arm extended.

"Tomorrow," he said without turning. "Try to get some rest. I'll be back early."

He was gone before she could argue. Before she could plead.

Alone again, Mia propped her hips on the edge of the bed, fighting back the desperation. The humiliation.

Maybe he was right. Maybe they were all right, and she'd imagined someone else with her on the bluff. A sinister shadow behind her.

Three hundred and ten days, she thought, her eyes welling with tears. She'd had three hundred and ten good days.

And tomorrow, she'd have to start over again at one.

Chapter 3

Ty felt like a heel as he left the Eternal Emergency Care Clinic. Not because he'd admitted Mia Serrat for overnight observation when she so clearly wanted to go home—standard procedure was standard procedure, and he dared follow nothing *but* when the patient was Karl Serrat's niece. There was also her son's safety to think about.

What troubled him was the niggle of pleasure he'd felt at the knowledge that, by admitting her, he'd have to see her again in the morning.

She was a patient, for Christ's sake. He knew better than to think of her in any other terms.

She was also a woman, though. A spirited, strong-willed, self-reliant woman.

Exactly the kind of woman he liked.

Shivering, he turned the heater on full blast in his ancient VW Beetle and pulled out onto Highway 18 toward Belier. Snow swirled furiously around his little car, falling faster now than when he'd driven in, and whipped into a frenzy by a fierce north wind. Windshield wipers and headlights hardly penetrated the miasma.

He leaned forward, peering into the blizzard to make out the road, but instead he kept seeing her defiant green eyes, the determined set to her full lips.

He shook his head at himself. Mia Serrat was completely off-limits.

She also had a history of mental illness. She'd backed off her story about being pushed off the bluff this morning without argument, but she wasn't convinced. He could see it in her eyes. She just knew the psychiatry game well enough to know better than to sound paranoid.

The sooner she was out of his life, the better.

Still, she pulled at him on a lot of different levels. Sure, she was beautiful. But she'd also overcome a lot of tragedy. She was a survivor, Mia Serrat. No way a woman trying to pick out a Christmas present for her kid had tried to kill herself. Suicidal people didn't make plans for a future they wouldn't be around to see.

On his left a steep rock wall angled back from the roadway. He slowed, squinting up at what he could see of Shilling's Bluff. On impulse he swerved to the shoulder, parked and got out for a closer look.

More than the cold made him shiver as he stared up at the rough slope. How the hell had she come down that and into a busy road without being seriously hurt?

Killed.

It would, he thought, be a good place to kill someone.

He crossed the road and found a trail in the woods to one side of the bluff. Without stopping to question why, he climbed to the top.

He knelt. Lots of footprints in the snow here. Rounded and shallow as the wind smoothed off the edges and new snow filled the impressions, but definitely more than one person's prints. Someone could have waited. Hidden in the trees—

His cell phone chirped, nearly sending him headfirst over the edge of the cliff.

He stood and turned away from the precipice to answer. His mother's voice screeched at him across the line.

"Ty-baby? Is that you? You sound like you're sitting on the wing of an airplane."

He capped one ear with his hand. "I'm outside, Ma. It's windy."

"Outside?" she chattered. "In this weather? You'll catch your death. What are you doing outside?"

He looked over his shoulder at the bluff, the nothingness beyond. What the hell *was* he doing? Trying to prove that Mia Serrat was as stable as she seemed? That she hadn't imagined someone pushing her?

Or trying to eliminate one of his reasons for keeping her at arm's length?

He swore and pulled his collar up as he started back toward his car. It was friggin' freezing out here. Sure there were lots of footprints. The sheriff's deputies would have checked out the scene after the accident.

"I'm headed back in, Ma. What did you need?"

He could hear Beethoven's Fifth playing in the background. It always played in the background.

"I was thinking you could come see me this weekend," she said, her voice more like a child's than a mother's now. "Maybe stay a little longer, even."

His shoulders tensed. "I have a lot of work, Ma. Besides, you have an appointment with Dr. Calvin."

"You're a doctor. You can look after me."

His free hand fisted in the pocket of his coat. He struggled to keep his voice steady. "I'm a resident, Ma. You know what that means? It means I have no life. No time. It means if I don't keep my mind one-hundred-percent on the job, I might never be a doctor for real. Do you understand?"

"I could cook for you." Her voice took on a dreamy tone. "I bet you haven't had a decent meal in months. Do you remember when we used to make cookies together? I'd mix the batter and you'd lick the bowl?"

Ty bit his tongue. She'd never baked cookies for him in his life. Much less fixed him a decent meal. But she didn't know that. She thought all her little imaginings were fact.

For a moment, he almost wished it were true—

that his childhood had been idyllic. That he'd been her golden child and she'd been his storybook-perfect mother.

Only for a moment, though. If his mom hadn't been the way she was when he was a kid, he wouldn't have become the man he was now. What better motivation was there for becoming a psychiatrist than growing up in the clutches of a crazy mother?

Intellectually, he knew that her psychosis was a disease, an illness she hadn't asked for and couldn't prevent, but as a kid he'd only known the effect, not the cause. He'd known her mood swings, her temper. His mother had been sick, but too often, he'd been the one to suffer.

And yet, she was still his mother. He'd never been able to turn his back on her. Not completely. He closed his eyes. "Sure, we can do it again sometime," he said softly. "But not right now, okay? I just don't have time to b—"

He stopped himself just short of saying *babysit*.

"—to be with you. I should have a break around the end of the month. I'll drive out for the day."

"Only for a day? But I miss you, My Ty."

He reached his car and ratcheted the door open with numb fingers. His stomach tightened. The assisted-living complex she lived in was only about ten miles from here. She was his mother, and she was lonely.

He was a doctor and he had responsibilities. He had patients to see and a whole caseload of patient files to update before 8:00 a.m.

"Look, Ma, I gotta go," he said, ashamed to feel grateful for the Kaiser's last-minute assignment, but grateful all the same. He just didn't have the time, or the mental energy. Not right now. "I'll try to get out there next week."

He hung up without waiting for her acknowledgment. He folded himself into his car, blew on his hands and rubbed them together, wishing he could warm the cold knot of guilt in his chest as easily as he could warm his frozen fingers.

He started the car.

He'd give her a call and have a long chat when he got a break tomorrow, he promised himself.

Day after that, at the latest.

Mia jogged along the trail at the top of the bluff, her muscles burning, blood singing, breath puffing in front of her face. The view was beautiful from up here. The snow on the trees, the roads winding toward the valley, the village—

A hand hit her in the back. She felt the impression of the palm distinctly. Five fingers.

Falling. Pounding against rocks. Grating against frozen earth. Pavement—

Mia lurched to wakefulness, her heart pounding.

But she wasn't on Shilling's Bluff. Wasn't falling into the road with a pickup truck bearing down on her.

She was in her hospital room. In the dark.

Her mouth was dry, so she sat up to search the bedside table for water. She could make out a chair beside the bed and a monitor—not active, thank goodness—on a cart across the room. A slice of light angled in through a narrow window on the door.

Her heart stalled, then raced as she stared at the door. She couldn't see the handle.

She had to know.

Silently she slipped out of bed and padded into the light. Holding her breath she reached for the doorknob and turned it.

Not locked.

Her breath exploded in relief. For a minute she'd thought…

But, no. Thankfully, she'd been wrong. It wasn't locked.

She should go back to bed. There was no reason to worry. She wasn't a prisoner here, she hadn't been involuntarily committed. She'd agreed—albeit with little real choice in the matter—to stay for observation of her own accord. In the morning, she'd make nice with Dr. Handsome and be on her way. She had to be calm. Composed.

Rational.

Unfortunately there was nothing rational about the fear skittering up her spinal column like a monkey on a vine. Or about her growing certainty that her fall hadn't been an accident, despite what anyone else thought.

She hadn't slipped; she'd been pushed.

Was she losing it again? Going crazy?

She couldn't. Wouldn't let herself.

She glanced at the bed, but the restlessness inside her wouldn't let her sleep. What was the point of lying there and worrying?

She raised up on her toes and looked out the narrow window in the door. The nurses' station down the hall sat abandoned. Silently she pushed the door open and padded toward the desk. Maybe her medical chart would hold some clue as to what had really happened. At the very least it would tell her what the doctors—Ty Hansen, in particular—were thinking about her.

Tightening the drawstring on her yellow flannel pajamas, she shuffled over to the cluttered workstation. On the upper level of the desk area, coffee rings topped untidy stacks of folders. Yellow sticky notes and phone message slips papered the lower tier.

Mia fingered the files until she found what she was looking for. She scanned the pages quickly. History of depression. Prior commitment to a mental-health facility. Mother-in-law concerned about her current state of mind.

What?

Oh, Nana…

Before she had a chance to read exactly what Nana had told the doctor, a shuffling sound around the corner caught her attention.

Footsteps.

Fear paralyzed her until it was too late to scurry back to her room unseen. She wouldn't have worried about being caught by a nurse or orderly, but these footsteps didn't sound as if they belonged to a hospital employee. They were too slow, too measured.

It seemed almost as if the person around the corner was sneaking down the hallway. Toward her.

Maybe she really was paranoid. She debated standing her ground, but gave in to fear, the memory of this morning's shove firm in her mind— and on her back.

Out of time, she ducked behind the nurses' counter. The footsteps shuffled slowly closer, but didn't turn at the intersection of the two hallways. Instead they moved forward.

Toward the door to her room.

Heart thundering so loudly she thought surely whoever was out there would hear it, she raised up high enough to peek over the counter.

A slight man in baggy black sweatpants and an oversized black jacket stood outside her door. He looked over his shoulder as if to check whether he'd been seen. The hooded jacket hid his face, but Mia saw menace in the stoop of his shoulders, his careful step.

She held her breath as he pulled a vial out of his pocket. He uncapped a syringe with his mouth, drew the contents from the vial and tapped the bubbles to the top of the syringe. When he turned to check over his shoulder one more time, Mia ducked again.

That was no doctor. Even if it was, Dr. Hansen said she wasn't to be medicated.

A feeling that something was very, very wrong crept

over her. The intruder turned his back to her and flattened a hand on the door to her room, easing it open.

She hugged the wall with her back, then slid sideways, away from her room. Away from that man.

She was just about to turn the corner when her foot connected with the ball on a rolling chair. The chair clattered and crashed into the desk.

The intruder turned.

Mia gave in to panic and ran. Her bare feet slapped the cold tile, her footsteps in synch with the squeak of the intruder's sneakers as he followed her. She banged open the door to an emergency stairway and launched herself toward the ground floor.

Even as she ran she realized she should scream. Find someone to help her. But the sound froze in her throat.

She'd screamed before. No one had heard her. Or if they had, they hadn't cared.

The Eternal Emergency Care Clinic operated overnight with a skeleton staff. Most patients in need of extended treatment transferred to larger hospitals in Belier or Kyacy. Rarely did a patient stay overnight.

The building was virtually empty, except for her and a man with a syringe.

Mia ran faster.

The door to the stairwell clacked open behind her. Footsteps matched her hurried descent. She stopped at the ground floor and pushed through the exit.

A blast of frigid air hit her like a slap in the face. She had no way of knowing what time it was, but it was still dark. In the distance, a single streetlight lit the empty parking area. Drifting snow danced in its glow.

Mia backed inside the building and let the door close. She couldn't go out there. She had no coat, no shoes. The parking lot was empty, the street deserted. Who knew how far she would have to run before she found help in a sleepy little village like Eternal?

A hysterical laugh bubbled out of her. She might be crazy, but she wasn't stupid.

Hugging herself, she hurried down the final flight of stairs to what appeared to be the basement. There was no sign of the man chasing her, but he was coming. She could feel it. Gooseflesh bubbled on her skin.

Maybe she had imagined it, the way she had imagined someone pushing her on the bluff.

Somewhere above her, a door creaked open.

Giving in to her dread, she raced through a door marked *Cafeteria*. She yanked open drawers in the empty kitchen until she found a knife and then settled herself between a huge stainless-steel double sink and a stand of metal shelves.

She didn't know who was after her, or why. If he really even existed or if he was a figment of her imagination, a bump on the head and medication.

But real or not, she was going to be ready.

Chapter 4

About the time he pulled into the parking lot of the Eternal Emergency Care Clinic, Ty could have used a couple of toothpicks to hold his eyelids up. With the help of two pots of coffee and a Red Bull, he'd managed to land his updated patient-care charts in the Kaiser's inbox just shy of 6:00 a.m. The winds had died down since last night and the snowplows had cleared the roads, so he'd made good time from Belier. Now all he had to do was give the good Ms. Serrat the once-over—professionally speaking, of course—and send her on her way, and with any luck her uncle Karl would have no cause to send his career down in flames.

This week.

Maybe he'd even get in a little catnap before his shift at the hospital.

A sheriff's cruiser sat cockeyed in front of the employee entrance. Funny. He'd noticed another out front.

His guard was up a little, and the difference in atmosphere struck him like a slap when he walked into the corridor. Groups of orderlies huddled in the hall, their eyes darting back and forth as they whispered. A couple of pale-faced nurses tapped anxiously on each door as they moved away from Ty, opening and entering each room before coming back out and shaking their heads. A uniformed deputy strolled along behind, a hint of boredom barely showing beneath his stone-faced expression.

Ty tapped a nurse he recognized from last night on the shoulder. "What's going on?"

She grabbed him by the elbows. "Oh, thank God you're here. We've lost your patient."

"What do you mean, lost her?"

"I mean she's gone. Her bed was empty when the floor nurse went in for morning rounds."

The blood drained from Ty's head. "Have you called her family? Maybe she skipped out and went home."

"We checked. They haven't seen her. Her mother-in-law and uncle are on their way here."

Great. Maybe he'd been premature in his prediction that his career would last another week.

"She can't have gone far," the nurse continued.

"Her clothes and shoes are still in the closet in her room. She has to be in the building somewhere."

Reflexively, Ty stole a glance out the glass door at the snow beyond and shivered. The mentally ill sometimes didn't feel physical discomfort until it was too late. If she had left the building…

He threw his coat over the nurses' counter and raked a hand through his uncombed hair. "All right. What areas have you searched so far?"

"Her whole floor. The common areas on other floors, waiting rooms, doctors' lounges and such. The main lobby and the second-floor patient rooms."

"So that leaves intensive care—I doubt she's there, there are enough staff around someone would have noticed—the first-floor patient rooms and the basement."

"We just sent a group to the first floor to look. The graveyard shift stayed over to search, and the morning crew is helping out, too. Everyone we can spare. They've got all the main floors covered."

"Guess that leaves us with the basement, then."

He gestured toward the stairwell and strode off after her. At least he wasn't sleepy any longer. Amazing what a jolt of adrenaline could do to the human body.

The high he was riding didn't subside, even after twenty minutes of searching for his wayward patient.

There was only one area left to search down here—the kitchen. Ahead a faint gruelish smell filtered around a stainless-steel swinging door.

He threw a glance at Nurse Renee. "Let's go."

His heart sank when they walked into the kitchen. A couple of cooks in grease-stained white aprons shuffled about, clanging pots and pans. Mia couldn't be here; she would have been spotted. Maybe she really had left the building, in which case she was out in the snow, coatless and shoeless somewhere. He'd seen stranger things as a psychiatrist, but none had given him quite the same feeling of dread as picturing Mia shivering and alone did now.

"Mia?" he called out, helplessness loud and clear in his voice.

The cooks stopped and stared at him.

He walked down the aisle between stoves and sinks, looking left and right, studying. Ahead, the kitchen bent around in a narrow L shape. A row of stainless-steel cutting tables and cabinets lined one side of the room.

From beneath one of the tables, five bare toes wiggled against the tile floor.

"Mia?" Barely aware of the nurse jogging behind him, Ty hurried to where Mia sat huddled on the floor, but made himself slow down before he squatted next to her. He didn't want to startle her.

When he did lower himself to her level, he was the one who startled.

Both hands wrapped around the handle, she clasped a butcher knife against her chest.

Though his heart thundered in his chest, he forced a professional calm into his voice. "Hey, what'cha doing down here?"

She blinked, her eyes vacant.

"Mia? Are you okay?"

This time he got a twitch out of her. A tiny sign of recognition.

"Can you tell me what you're doing here?" He made no move toward her. Not with that knife so close to her heart.

Her lips trembled. "There was a… There was a man."

"A man where?"

"In my room."

"In your hospital room? Upstairs?"

She nodded, the movement jerky. At least he could see her breathing now, and a spot of color had returned to her cheeks.

"Who was it?"

"I don't know. He was dressed all in black. He had a hood." Her gaze jumped up to his, suddenly electric. "He was going to hurt me."

Damn. How could he have been so wrong about her? She'd seemed so stable yesterday, despite her confusion about being pushed down the bluff. That could be written off as a normal defensive mechanism. He wanted to write it off.

He wanted her to be normal.

But the paranoid delusion she described was anything but normal. Hiding beneath a stainless-steel counter with a butcher knife before dawn was anything but normal.

A knot tightened in his chest as he realized how

long and painful the road to recovery would be for a person with an illness like this. And not just for her, but for her family, too. She had a son, she'd said.

"Mia, why don't you put down the knife and we can talk about it, okay?"

Confusion clouded her green eyes. She glanced down, and looked at the weapon she held as if she'd never seen it before, hadn't realized she held it. Her eyes went wide. The blade clattered to the floor.

Moving slowly, Nurse Renee leaned in and slid it away.

"There, that's better." Ty slowly raised his hand toward Mia. She hesitated to take his hand, to trust him, but he waited out her reluctance. Her shock.

What he wouldn't give for a shower and a clean shirt. Yesterday's clothes were getting a little ripe. He wouldn't be leaving here for some time, though. When he did go, Mia Serrat would be going back to the Massachusetts Hospital of Mental Health with him—as a patient.

And she knew it—her green eyes had gone so dark they were almost black. He steeled himself against the urge to comfort her, to tell her everything would be all right. She had to face her illness, and he had to help her do it.

This was why he'd gotten into medicine. Into psychiatry. Because of people like Mia. People like his mother. Good people who needed help.

He just hadn't known how it would eat his gut.

"Come on," he urged. "Why don't we go somewhere a little more comfortable and you can tell me what happened?"

Ten minutes later, Mia was tucked back between her covers with a mug of steaming tea and Dr. Handsome was perched on a stool next to the bed.

"You don't believe me," she said flatly.

"I'm just trying to understand—"

"Huh." She gulped a mouthful of air. "Don't give me the psychobabble. I've heard it all before."

He raked a hand through his hair and stretched his back. "Okay, why do you think someone would want to hurt you?"

She cut him a sideways glance. "Oh, now you believe there is a man?"

"Just go with me here."

She sighed, a wistful breath of air that rippled the tea. The steam above the mug swirled. "I don't know."

"Did he say anything?"

"No. He didn't see me. Not at first."

"How could he not see you?"

"I wasn't in my room. I was in the hall…. Oh, what's the use."

"No, go ahead. You were in the hall."

She blew on her tea and took a sip. "He stopped outside my door and looked around like, to see if anyone was watching."

The doctor scrubbed his hands over his face. He looked tired, and he was wearing the same clothes he'd had on yesterday. "Are you sure it wasn't a doctor? You were tired and had hit your head. Maybe you just thought—"

"How many doctors do you know that wear black hoodies pulled way up over their faces when they're making rounds?"

"So you're basing your assumption that someone is trying to kill you on one person's bad choice of clothing?"

"He pulled a syringe out of his pocket!" She set her tea on the bedside table and crossed her arms over her chest. "Didn't you tell me you left orders that I wasn't to be given any medications so that you could clear me for release in the morning?"

He just stared at her, his eyes unreadable. Tired, but unreadable. The *doctor* look. She hated it.

"Fine," she spat out and threw her head back on the pillow. "It was all my imagination."

"Stop."

"Stop what?"

"Telling me what you think I want to hear."

"Well you didn't seem too pleased to hear the truth."

"That someone is trying to kill you."

"Well I'm not going to say that I was trying to kill myself."

"I found you holding a knife to your chest."

"For *protection!* Someone tried to kill me twice in one day!"

He frowned. "You said you slipped and fell off the bluff."

"*Then,* I was telling you what you wanted to hear. *Now,* I'm telling you the truth."

"How am I supposed to know which is the truth and which is the lie?"

She gritted her teeth, clenched her fists and groaned, then sank back against the bed, deflated. "Shrinks."

He opened his mouth. She cut him off fast and hard. "Don't you dare ask me how I *feel* about shrinks."

He feigned innocence. "I was going to ask you if you'd like some more tea. Yours is cold by now."

Terrific. A little humiliation to go with her mortification.

"No, thank you."

He straightened and took a deep breath. She braced herself—she knew what that meant.

"Look, I think you should come to the MHMH for a few days. Straighten out in your head what really happened and didn't happen yesterday and last night."

Someone had dropped a bowling ball on her stomach. "No!"

He reached over and covered her clenched hand with his. His palm was warm, slightly rough. She jerked from beneath his touch.

"I'm afraid I have to insist," he said.

She bolted upright in bed. She'd known this was coming, and still she wasn't prepared. "You can't do this!"

"On the contrary." He stood, his shoulders rounded. "It's my job to do this, whether I like it or not." The expression on his face made her believe that in this case, he definitely did not. It was small comfort.

Every nerve in her body jumped. She was on fire. She licked her lips. "Look, you're probably right. I slipped and fell on the bluff. And last night, I—I had a headache and I don't sleep well in hospitals. It was probably just a nightmare. I didn't really see anything at all. I overreacted a little."

He stopped at the door. "I really hope that's all it was. But I have to be sure." His lips pressed together. "Not just for your sake, but for your son's."

If there was one thing in the world he could have said that would set her back, make her think about what was happening to her, that was it.

Her son.

If there really was something wrong with her, it wasn't Todd's fault. From the moment he'd been born, she'd vowed to protect him. Protect him she would—even if it was from herself.

Tears welled in her eyes. Dr. Handsome stayed in the door, looking torn.

"We'll work it out," he said quietly. "Don't give up."

Then he was gone.

Work it out? Hell, what was there to work out if she was losing her mind?

Chapter 5

Ty slapped the vending machine on the side trying to eke a few more drops of stale coffee into the paper cup.

"They're waiting for you," Nurse Renee said from behind.

He grabbed the cup, downed half, and turned. "I know."

She grimaced. "How do you think they're going to take the news?"

"Oh, about like a bad case of the stomach flu."

"Don't let Dr. Serrat get to you. He treats everyone like crap. He's not a happy man."

"Yeah." Ty headed for the door to the conference room, stopped just outside. Karl Serrat was definitely not a happy man, and Ty had a feeling he was about to make him a lot unhappier.

The Kaiser sat stiffly at the head of a scarred work table. Beside him, an older woman he recognized from the night before as Mia's mother-in-law, Nana, fidgeted in her chair. Her short gray hair curled neatly around her head, but her face was as crumpled as the tissue she wrung in her aged hands. A woman about Ty's age sat between the two Serrats, wavy red hair pulled back in a ponytail and just a smidge too much makeup.

"Ma'am," he nodded toward the older woman.

"My niece Citria," Karl introduced, gesturing toward the younger female. "Mia's sister-in-law."

Ty hadn't known Karl had a niece, or a sister for that matter. Then again, it wasn't like the two of them sat around drinking beer and talking over a hand of cards on Saturday nights.

Karl folded his hands on the tabletop. "I've filled in my sister and Citria on Mia's condition from your report last night and what the hospital staff told me this morning. What do you have to add?"

Ty took a moment to study the faces in front of him before answering. Karl sounded almost blasé. Not at all the belligerent defense of a family member he'd expected. The man had to know where this was going.

Nana seemed appropriately concerned, her eyes welling and hands clutching that ragged tissue. Citria mirrored Nana's worry, but there was something a bit more…saccharine in the expression.

Strange family.

"Mia has had two delusional episodes," he said carefully, waiting for an explosion that never came. "She believes someone is trying to kill her."

"Oh." Nana dabbed at her eyes. "I should have seen this coming. I knew something was wrong. I knew it wasn't right."

"What wasn't right?" Ty asked.

"She was talking about leaving. Why would she want to leave? Take Todd away?"

"Did she say why she wanted to leave?"

"Just that it was time. She needed to get back on her feet. She wasn't ready. I told her she wasn't ready."

Citria rubbed her mother's forearm. "It's not your fault, Mom."

Nana shook her head. "I should have known."

"Your daughter's right, ma'am. It's not your fault. Sometimes these illnesses reappear without warning, or the warnings are so subtle they're easy to miss. Did Mia ever give any indication that she wanted to leave because she was afraid of something here? Because she thought someone was watching or stalking her?" he asked, trying to confirm the onset of paranoia.

"No. No, nothing like that. Do you think she made up those stories because she didn't want us to know she tried to hurt herself again?"

"It's possible," Ty said. "But I got the feeling that she really believed what she was saying."

"So what is your recommendation, Doctor?"

Ty resisted the urge to squirm at Karl's question.

He looked squarely at the man who held his career in his hands. "Mandatory seventy-two-hour commitment to a mental-health facility for full evaluation."

"Based on what criteria?" Karl knew the drill damn well. But it would be unethical for him to make a psychological evaluation on a member of his family. He needed an independent opinion, thus putting Ty smack between a rock and a hard place.

"She is a potential danger to herself and her son."

"Mia would never hurt Todd," Nana chimed in.

Citria didn't look so convinced. "Mom, we can't take the chance."

"We don't know the extent of her delusions," he explained. "She could mistake him for her assailant at some point. Or if she believes she is being attacked and he is nearby, she could actually hurt him in a misguided attempt to protect him. What if, for instance, she thinks she's being chased by a car, and she drives recklessly while Todd is with her, thinking she needs to escape? We really need to get a handle on the extent of her delusions, and the best way to do that is to control her environment, keep her under observation."

Silence lay heavy in the room. Karl finally spoke up. "We agree. We have a judge faxing over the papers now."

Ty's heart bounced. He'd expected a fight. Most families weren't generally so quick to accept that their loved one needed that kind of intense help. But then, most families weren't the Serrats.

* * *

Mia soaked in the scenery as the ambulance ambled up the winding drive to the Massachusetts Hospital of Mental Health, knowing it would be the last she'd see of sunshine for a while. Her stomach turned, and she fought in vain to tamp down the fear. Locked doors, cries rolling up and down the hallway in the night, walls that seemed always to be closing in on her. Those were the memories of her first days at the California hospital where she'd been confined for eighteen months.

Later she had to admit this place didn't look quite so bad. The fence outside was brick and wrought iron, made to look ornamental from the outside, but still tall and sturdy enough to discourage climbing from the inside. The corridor walls were painted pastel yellows, greens and blues instead of austere white, and fresh flowers sat on small tables outside each patient room.

Mia was led to room 213. Inside she found an old-fashioned spindle bed with a soft chenille cover, a marble-topped dresser and a wicker rocking chair in the corner. It would have passed for a guest room in a quaint bed-and-breakfast if it wasn't for the wire mesh over the window.

The orderly in purple scrubs who had shown her to her room lifted the bag Nana had packed for her. "I'll have this back in a flash."

Mia nodded. She knew the drill. They'd take her shoelaces, the compact from her makeup case because it contained a little glass mirror. Anything that could possibly be used to hang, cut, poison or otherwise do herself in. She supposed it was necessary, but that made it no less humiliating.

She flinched when the door snicked shut behind her, and then lowered herself into the rocker to wait. One of the first things a patient gave up in a place like this was control of her schedule. She would eat when they told her, go to bed when they told her, see the doctors at her assigned time. Resistance was futile.

The wicker creaked as she swung slowly forward and back. On the table next to her was a small book of poetry. Not the heavy, dreary stuff, but a collection of silly little rhymes.

Mia smiled as she turned page after page, thinking how much Todd would like the limericks. Maybe she'd ask if she could take it when she left in a few days.

If she left.

Floor nurse Nancy Popadopalous's curly black hair bobbed into view over Ty's shoulder as he leaned a hip on her desk, flipping through patient charts. He'd finally had a shower, shave and a change of clothes. He felt almost human. Now he just needed to read through staff notes on what had been happening with his patients and prioritize twelve hours' worth of work into the six hours left in his day.

In reality, he already knew what his priority was. She should be settled in her room by now. She was a puzzle he needed to solve—how a person who appeared to be so together could fall apart so completely. But first, he had a responsibility to the twenty-two other patients in his care.

Nancy poked him with her pen. "Get your butt off my desk, hotshot."

"Sorry," he mumbled, standing.

"Heard you drew the short straw."

"Huh?"

"Got Mia Serrat as a patient."

He looked up. "Yeah, you know her?"

"No. My son Scott goes to school with her son, though. Heard she downed a whole bottle of phenobarb a couple of years back. Man, I can't imagine taking on the Kaiser's niece as a patient. Talk about pressure—you screw up, or just piss him off, you're toast."

"Thanks for the pep talk, Nance."

"I'm just sayin'…"

"Yeah, yeah. So maybe you help me stay untoasted? Request her files from California. The family will sign the consent."

He left Nancy cracking her knuckles as she booted up her computer and strode down the hall with a stack of charts under his arm and a pen between his teeth.

Three hours later, he'd seen the most urgent of his patients, rescheduled the therapy sessions he'd missed this morning, and finally gave in to the need to check on Mia.

Peeking through the small window on her door, he saw her sitting cross-legged in the wicker chair, her head sagging and a book slipping off her lap. For a moment his pulse leaped, sure something was wrong, but he realized when he opened the door that she was sound asleep.

He watched her unabashedly, enjoying the occasional soft snuffling sound and the way her lashes fluttered. In her sleep, she looked vigorous, happy, healthy, the way a young mother in her prime should. There was no sign of the malignancy within her. She was so different from many of the patients he saw, from his own mother, whose face had twisted in misery even in sleep.

She didn't belong here. This place would eat her alive, steal that vitality bit by bit. He'd seen it happen too many times already, even in his brief career. Hospitals were supposed to help, but so often the isolation and the fact of being surrounded by a population of the mentally ill only seemed to make people worse.

His hope to help her hardened to resolve. He had to help her, had to help her get back what she'd lost.

And that was a slippery slope, professionally.

How many lectures had he sat through on the importance of professional detachment?

Quietly Ty pulled the cover off the twin bed against the wall and tucked the spread around her, pausing to sweep a lock of dark hair away from the corner of her mouth.

She was a picture, a painting. She rubbed her cheek against his hand as he pulled it away.

How was he supposed to detach from that?

As he walked out of the room, Nancy stopped him. How long had she been standing there?

"Those records are on the way. They promised to e-mail them within the next hour."

"Thanks, Nance."

He headed to the office to log on to the computer. It looked like it was going to be another long night.

"Let the interrogation begin!" Mia greeted Ty cheerily from the door to his office. It was smaller than she'd expected, and a little dingy, with worn carpeting and folders stacked a foot deep on his metal desk. Her room was nicer than this.

"Ah, there it is!" he called back just as cheekily.

She frowned. "What?"

"That moxie of yours. I missed it this morning."

"Moxie?"

"You know. Chutzpah. Courage."

She edged into the room. "You think I have courage?"

"Yup. And this isn't an interrogation room."

"Isn't it where I stretch out on your couch—" She glanced around his dismal domain. "Which you seem to be missing, by the way. And you grill me about my domineering father, my submissive mother and how I *feel* about everything from global warming to rap music?"

How on earth did he cure the infirmed without a leather couch?

He picked a coat off the back of his chair—the coat that had been taken from her at the front door yesterday—and threw it at her. "Actually, this is where we take a walk."

She blinked. "Really?"

"You're a runner, right? Figured you'd appreciate a little exercise. I'd jog with you, but I'm afraid I'd collapse before we made it around the building."

What was it about him that he knew exactly how to throw her off balance? "And here I came with sword in hand ready to do battle, and you're being nice," she said.

"Nice is bad?" He grabbed his own beat-up leather coat and ushered her out the door.

"No," she admitted. "Nice is good."

Nice was really, really good when she got outside and filled her lungs with fresh, crisp air.

They walked in silence awhile, meandering down a path that had been blown clear of snow. A few hardy birds flitted among the fir trees and sun blazed off a crystal-blue pond not yet frozen over at the bottom of the hill.

"Are you really not going to ask me any questions?" she finally blurted.

He gave her an innocent look that was pure mischief. She should recognize the boyish expression. She'd seen it a thousand times on Todd's face.

"What should I ask?"

"Very clever. Making me set the agenda."

"I'm serious. What do I need to know about you?"

There he went again, upsetting her equilibrium. "That I'm not crazy?" she tried.

"I never said you were."

"I have no desire to hurt myself."

"That's good."

She stopped. "You are infuriating, you know that?"

He nudged her along, toward the pond. "How so?"

"You're not following the rules. You're supposed to ask stupid probing questions and I'm supposed to dodge them."

One corner of his mouth quirked up. "Look, you've been through this before. It's obvious you had a doctor who was not, shall we say, very creative in his therapeutic technique. I'm just trying a different technique."

"What technique would that be?"

"Getting to know you."

Whammo! Not just off balance, but knocked on her butt.

"You want to know me?"

He shrugged. "Sure, why not? You seem like an interesting person."

"I'm just used to doctors who would rather dissect me."

"Like I said…not very creative."

"Or sincere," she added, and looked at him quizzically. "So if you get to know me, and I turn out to be a pretty normal, okay kind of person, are you going to break me out of this nuthouse and let me get back to my life?"

"That's the goal, yes."

"The goal, but not the plan."

"I don't have a plan. We're working on your agenda, remember?"

"My agenda is to get home."

"You've made that clear."

She studied him as they walked. He had a good face. Not classically handsome, but kind eyes, a strong jaw. A little white scar beneath his lower lip to remind her that boys will be boys.

"All rightie, then. Getting to know me. I'm five foot eight, one hundred and twenty-eight pounds. I wear a size-eight shoe and my favorite comfort food is macaroni and cheese. I pretend it's a treat for Todd when I make it for Saturday lunch, but really it's for me. What about you?"

"What about me?" He jammed his hands in the pockets of his jacket.

"My agenda, right? If I'm going to tell you all my secrets, I want to know something about you, too. Turnabout is fair play."

"Hmm." He jammed his hands in the pockets of his jacket as he mulled it over. "I suppose. I'm five foot eleven and a half—it always pissed me off that I never hit six foot. A hundred and seventy-eight pounds and I wear a size nine. Good enough?"

"Stat sheet. What about the good stuff?"

"Right, comfort food. Sushi."

She made a gagging sound. "You're kidding."

"Nope. Seaweed and raw fish. Gotta love it."

"My husband liked sushi. He dragged me along whenever he found a new place, always insisting I'd find something on the menu I would like."

She wondered if he'd known about Sam's sushi

taste somehow, and was devious enough to use the little details of her married life to get inside her head.

"Did you? Find something?"

"Every time." She grinned. "The sake."

"Ah, the liquid diet."

"What else do you want to know about me?" She found herself surprisingly willing to tell him. He was disarming that way.

"No questions, remember? You decide what we talk about."

She sighed. "All right, let's get to the meat of it, then. A few years ago, I was feeling pretty down because I'd lost my blood family. My mom, dad and sister were all gone. Then Sam was killed in a car accident on Highway 1, took a curve too fast in the dark and drove right into the ocean, they said. All of a sudden, the lone-liness was overwhelming. I started to have a hard time doing the simplest things, like making the bed or reading Todd a story. That was the hardest part, knowing that I wasn't giving my son what he needed. He'd lost his dad, and now it was like his mom was just fading away. I felt…transparent. And the more pressure I put on myself to get with it, the guiltier I felt when I failed. Eventually I just gave up. Trying was too painful, so I sent Todd off to day camp and swallowed a bottle of pills. I didn't even know what I was taking."

She shook her head. "Now it all seems like a dream—a nightmare really—or a story I read or something. It doesn't seem real. Even I can't under-stand why I did it, so I don't expect you to."

"I have a pretty good idea how desperate life can become when you're in constant pain."

She wasn't sure what that meant. Wasn't sure she wanted to know that much about him after all. He was her doctor, and she needed his professional support to end this latest nightmare.

"Luckily for me, I had totally forgotten my housekeeper was due that day. When I didn't answer the bell, she let herself in with her key and found me on the floor in the bedroom. She's the one who called 911."

"Maybe it wasn't really luck."

"You're saying it would have been better if Roberta hadn't been there?"

"Of course not. I'm saying sometimes our subconscious is smarter than our conscious mind. Maybe you didn't really forget that the housekeeper was due. Subconsciously you knew she'd find you. I'm saying you didn't really want to die."

"Maybe." She wasn't sure she believed that, but she'd take anything positive he offered. "I ended up in the hospital, as you know. For a while, I just felt sorry for myself, but eventually I knew I had to get out of there. I couldn't live like that. I worked hard and got my body and my mind healthy again. Despite my doctor's lack of creativity, I did everything he told me, everything he asked of me. He really was a good doctor, and in time, I got better. I did it for myself and for Todd. On the day I was discharged, I swore I'd never go back. I'd never let myself fall so far again. And I haven't. I don't want to kill myself, but apparently someone else out there does."

She tipped her chin defiantly, daring him to contradict her. He didn't.

More silence from him.

"It's okay. You can ask me questions now."

"Nope. I have a better idea."

She hooked one eyebrow at him.

"Let's head back inside. I want to get you some paper and a pen from the nurses' supply."

"What for?"

"You have a homework assignment. I want you to write down exactly what happened on the bluff and in the clinic in Eternal."

"Why?"

"So that we can give it to the police. If someone's trying to kill you, they should be investigating."

She stopped in her tracks. She just about had to pick her jaw up off the ground to talk. "You believe me?"

He kept walking ahead of her. "We'll see. Let's just get it all written down for now."

She jogged to catch up to him. Her pulse hammered in her veins. Could he really believe her? She hardly dared hope, yet she couldn't help herself.

Hope, it seemed, was as hard to kill as she was.

Chapter 6

"You're kidding, right?" Chuck Campbell, an old school friend who was now a senior corporal with the Fulmer County Sheriff's Department, shot Ty a look of disbelief.

"No. I want you to interview her."

Chuck laid the handwritten pages he'd just finished reading on the edge of Ty's desk, kicked back in his chair and put his boots up beside them. "Old buddy, you wouldn't be sending me on a wild-goose chase now, would you?"

"Would I do that to you?"

"Remember when we were in fifth grade and you told me you'd overheard a couple talking about burying a bag of money they'd stolen down by the old covered bridge? And then there was the time in junior high when you pretended to be a secret admirer and left a note in my locker saying you'd be waiting for me. Only the note just led to another note and so on. I spent all day chasing the wind."

"All right, all right." Ty waved his hand. "Can we focus here?" he said, though he was smiling, too. Those were the days…and he'd had precious few of them as a child.

Turning serious again, he chose his next words carefully. He was treading a fine ethical line here. "You know that by law I can't discuss the specifics of any illness Mia might or might not have."

"*Mia* now, is it?"

Ty ignored the insinuation. Mostly because it was true. "Or her treatment. But speaking in general terms, you can't just convince a delusional person that what they saw—or believe they saw—didn't happen, because to them, it did happen. It's that real to them."

"I get it. But if that's the case, what good is my interviewing her going to do?"

"First of all, it will reassure her that there are people who want to help her, that there are people who will listen."

"Isn't that just playing into her delusions?"

How did he explain a graduate course in psychotherapy in thirty seconds or less?

"I'm not saying every doctor would agree with the approach. But I believe that a patient like Mia—a patient—" he corrected himself, remembering this was supposed to be a hypothetical discussion "—who is smart and is generally grounded in reality will figure out that something isn't right about that false memory if they can take the emotion out of it."

Chuck pulled Mia's account of what had happened closer with his fingertips. "Like writing it down?"

"And telling it to a cop."

"I'm not a shrink, Ty."

"Good, because she's already got one of those."

"What if I make her worse? Screw her up?"

"Just get her to tell you what happened the way you would any witness. You don't have to tell her you believe her story, but don't belittle her for it, either. Just…keep an open mind."

Chuck sighed and dropped his feet off the desk. "Open mind. Right. Let's get this over with."

Ty followed him to the door, where the deputy stopped, leaning on the jamb. "This is just some weird witch-doctor ritual you're using to help this girl, right? You don't really think someone tried to kill her."

He didn't, he had to admit, if only to himself. He wanted to—even catching a would-be assassin seemed a less daunting task than curing a difficult mental disorder.

"I can't imagine why anyone would want to hurt her."

"Only three motives for murder—passion, power or money."

Ty shook his head. "Nothing's clicking for me. I

could ask around, talk to the family. If you think there's a chance—"

Chuck grinned. "Tell you what. You handle the witch-doctor rituals. Leave the detective work to me."

Sound advice, Ty figured, yet his mind wouldn't stop spinning those three little words. *Passion. Power. Money.*

He ruled out power. The one love of Mia's life—excepting her son—was gone. She didn't have power over much of anything. But money...

From what he'd read in her file, Mia Serrat had lots of money.

Mia jogged little circles around Ty. "Come on, just pick up your feet a little. Just a little bounce in the toes. You can do it."

"I prefer to walk, thank you." He sounded stern, but the wrinkles at the corner of his mouth gave him away. He'd shown up this morning and again in the evening at her door to get her. She had a feeling he enjoyed their walks almost as much as she did.

She stopped running and fell into step beside him. "Lazy."

He raised his right hand. "Flag-carrying, chest-thumping proud member of the lazy doctor club."

She pinched his bicep. Even through his leather jacket she could feel the firm bulge of muscle. "I doubt that."

"How did it go with Deputy Campbell this afternoon?"

"It was nice of him to pretend to take me seriously."

His frown told her she'd caught him off guard. "You don't think he believed you?"

"He's a friend of yours, right? The kind who couldn't turn you down no matter how crazy a favor you asked?"

"Perceptive little thing, aren't you?"

"Little thing?"

"Sorry. Perceptive young woman, aren't you? But friend or not, he's also a cop. Believe me, he takes attempted murder seriously."

She grinned up at him, suddenly wanting to laugh at him, at herself, at the whole ridiculous situation. The sun was going down across the pond, she was out of her little room, away from the disinfectant smell of the hospital, breathing clean air. If all went well, she only had one more night to spend in this place before she could go home.

"It's nice of you to pretend, too," she told him.

He walked in silence a few strides. His lack of an answer was an answer in itself.

"Have you thought any more about what happened?"

"You mean, do I still believe it happened?"

"Okay, now you're getting downright scary. I'm supposed to be the expert here."

This was the tough part of the conversation. The part she'd rehearsed in her mind all afternoon. "It all still seems very real to me, but I'll admit to the possibility that it could have been a clump of snow falling off a tree branch that hit me at the top of the bluff."

She'd admit to arriving on Earth in a capsule from Mars if it got her home to her son.

"And the man in the hospital, maybe it was just a dream. You know how real dreams can seem when you first wake up."

Had he bought it? Queen of stage and screen, she was not.

He narrowed his eyes at her. "Don't play me."

"This is no game."

"No," he said after studying her for a long moment. He pulled his coat tighter across his body. "Come on, let's head back. It'll be dark soon."

He walked her all the way to her room, then stood in the doorway as though they had unfinished business. If this had been a date, she would have thought he was deciding whether or not to kiss her.

Her cheeks immediately warmed at the silly thought. This was no date. She was no sweet-sixteener and he was no pimply-faced boy.

Her gaze lingered on the wide shoulders, then traveled the length of the slim hips and long, jeans-clad legs.

No, that was definitely not the body of a boy.

"Did you…want something else?" she asked.

"Mia." His eyes had darkened a shade, along with his expression.

She waited for him to continue.

"Yes?" she finally prompted.

His jerked a little as if he'd nearly fallen asleep—or had just woken from a daze—and cleared his throat.

"Nothing." He took a step back, out of her doorway. "I mean, good night."

She cocked her head. What in the world had gotten into him? "Good night."

When he was gone, she closed the door behind him and leaned her back against the cool steel.

Whatever it was, she'd felt it, too.

Ty stalked down the hospital hall, each step a little angrier than the one before.

What the hell had gotten into him?

He'd been about to ask her if she had a will. Who, besides Todd, would get her estate if she died.

And if he hadn't done that, he damned sure would have kissed her.

He'd nearly lost his mind, watching her stand there with her cheeks flushed from the cold and dark hair damp with melted snow, her chin tipped up, green eyes looking deeply into his. She was a patient. She was supposed to look weak and needy. Dependent on the big, bad doctor to save her.

Instead she'd looked strong. And desirable.

He was getting too close to her, losing his objectivity. The last thing she needed was for him to feed her paranoia by giving her a reason to think someone might want her dead.

On second thought, that was the second-to-last thing she needed. The last thing she needed was a doctor who was more interested in getting inside her body than inside her head.

Slumping down into the squeaky chair behind his desk, he lifted a pencil from the blotter and twirled it in his fingers.

One more day, he told himself. Barring a major breakdown before then, Mia would be released tomorrow. Even if he did suspect she was just telling him what he wanted to hear, her seventy-two-hour observation period ended without incident. He would recommend some ongoing counseling—with a different physician. He wouldn't see her again.

He'd lost his flipping mind.

Chuck Campbell shrugged, stretched against the back of his desk chair and cracked his sugar-free gum. He'd like to have the real stuff, but his dentist would give him hell if he came in with another cavity.

His shift had ended two hours ago, yet here he sat pecking away at the computer. He had to admit, he understood what intrigued Ty about Mia Serrat— and he didn't mean her looks, although they were plenty intriguing. Despite Ty's denial, Chuck didn't doubt that his old friend had noticed that, too.

She had a way of roping a man into her story, making it sound plausible.

It would probably turn out to be a wild-goose chase, just like he'd accused Ty of setting up, but what the hell. His wife was at one of those ladies' parties tonight, Tupperware or some such. He had a few hours to kill.

Maybe he'd just poke around a little more. See if someone out there really did have reason to want Mia Serrat dead.

Chapter 7

"Do you have your recommendation?" The Kaiser spoke without looking up from the yellow pad he was jotting notes on with hard, slashing strokes. The mahogany desk he sat behind was as dark as the man's expression. Everything in Karl Serrat's office was dark.

Ty pushed the folder across the desk, but Karl didn't look interested. Odd, since the patient file in question belonged to his own niece. Soon she would have completed her seventy-two hours of observation. It was decision time.

"Well, go ahead, then."

"Sir?"

"Your recommendation, Doctor." He swirled his pen in the air. "Let's hear it."

"I recommend she be released, sir."

Finally Karl Serrat looked up, met Ty's gaze with eyes deep-set in a square face wrinkled by time. "You're sure about that?"

"I'm sure," he said.

"She has a young son, you know."

"Todd. He's all she talks about."

"If you're wrong, you're putting them both in jeopardy."

Ty swallowed hard. He realized that. Still the bastard had to point that out, knowing Ty's history. As if it wasn't enough that a terrific young woman's life—not to mention his career—was at stake. And to up the stakes even more, Karl cast a pointed look at Ty's right forearm. The one with the scars.

Fury burned in Ty's chest. "I realize that," he said tightly. "Of course I recommend continued supervision. She should be under the care of a good therapist, someone to keep an eye on her."

Karl returned his attention to his legal pad. "Good, see that you do."

Huh?

"Do what?"

Karl looked over his glasses at Ty without raising his head. "Keep an eye on her."

Ty's stomach dropped. "Me?"

"Eternal is a small town. There aren't exactly doctors with your qualifications on every street corner."

Was that a compliment?

"Are you saying you aren't willing to continue her treatment?"

Oh, hell. Now what? Tell the Kaiser that he wasn't qualified to treat his niece because he wanted to jump her bones?

Buck up, Hansen. You're supposed to be a professional.

"No, of course not."

"Good. Recommendation approved. File the release paperwork."

Dismissed, Ty shuffled off down the hall to break the news to Mia.

"Pack your bag, you're going home," he told her.

She literally jumped for joy, spinning in the air and clapping her hands. When she finally came down, she was breathless. It was very becoming.

"My bag is already packed. I just need to call Nana to come pick me up."

"Whoa there." He checked his watch. "The court order was for seventy-two hours of observation. Technically that's not up until 5:00 p.m. You've got two and a half more hours."

The joy ran out of her like bathwater down the drain. "Five o'clock? But Todd's school is having its Christmas pageant today. He's in the play. It starts at three."

Crap.

He had to do this by the book. "I'm sorry."

"But—"

The pain instilled in the single word tore at him, but he steeled himself. He was her doctor, not her friend. "The order was signed by a judge, Mia. I have to follow it."

She took a deep breath, her head bowed. When she raised it, her green eyes blazed. "Fine. I have an idea. You take me to the pageant."

"Mia, I can't—"

"Seventy-two hours of observation, the order said. You're the primary observer. You can observe me there as well as here."

He rocked back on his heels. Technically she was correct. He had the authority to take her off the grounds if he deemed it beneficial to her mental health, and there was no doubt that being present for her son's pageant would do worlds of good for her psychologically.

Right back between the rock and the hard place.

He nodded and she beat him to the door, packed bag in hand.

They got to Bridge Elementary just as the choir's first carol ended, but found seats and settled in just in time for a screeching first-grade rendition of "Rudolph the Red-Nosed Reindeer."

Mia tried not to wince as she looked over at Ty to see if he'd stuck his fingers in his ears to save his hearing yet.

She felt bad for dragging him here. He didn't wear a wedding ring. She assumed he didn't have kids, although she didn't have any facts other than there hadn't been any pictures on his desk to base that assumption on. Bachelors didn't tend to be big on kiddy functions. He really was a good sport for bringing her, even if it was his fault for nitpicking the whole seventy-two-hour observation thing to begin with.

He leaned over and yelled in her ear to be heard over the din. "I thought you said this was a play."

"It's a pageant. There's singing and dancing and a play."

"Oh." He smiled stiffly and winced when the soprano soloist hit a particularly painful note. "Great."

Obviously not great, but he gamely turned his attention back to the stage anyway.

Mia scanned the crowd, and found Nana and Citria on the other side of the auditorium with pretty much the same expression as Ty's on their faces. She tried to catch their attention by waving, but got a gruff "Down in front!" from the large man with the camcorder behind her.

The room was alight with the smiles and beaming faces of proud parents. Flashes popped and cameras whirred. Fingers jumped up and pointed as moms and dads cried out, "There's Jimmy," or "Bobby," or "Katie."

Mia could hardly wait her turn. The play was last on the program, and though she enjoyed all the kids' performances, she couldn't wait to see her son.

More importantly, she couldn't wait for him to see her. To know that she hadn't let him down. That she'd kept her promise, was here to see him. That she was home.

Nervous energy vibrated in her veins. Her foot bounced on the floor and her hands gripped the arms of her chair with enough force to leave dents.

After what seemed an eternity, the dancing swans left the stage, the choir came back on, but stayed half to each side. The house lights dimmed, and the choir began butchering the theme to "Frosty the Snowman" as the curtain opened. Todd was playing the magician who lost the top hat that brought Frosty to life. She'd helped him learn his lines.

"There he is!" Mia moved her death grip from the arm of the chair to Ty's arm, pointing with her other hand.

How handsome he looked in his black pants, crisp white shirt and black jacket with tails. She and Nana had come up with the idea of adding tails to his Sunday suit to make it look more like a tuxedo themselves. They did add an air of magical mystery to his costume!

The choir was still singing. The play hadn't started yet, but the stage lights were slowly coming up. Once they did, Mia knew Todd would be blinded, unable to see her in the crowd.

She strained upward, not quite standing, but trying to make herself taller. He was scanning the crowd, probably looking for Nana. If he'd just turn this way a little farther…

"Hey lady, down in front!" the man behind gruffed again.

She threw a look over her shoulder at him. "Just a second. That's my son! The magician."

"Well whoop-dee-do-la. That's my daughter, in the rabbit suit, and you're blocking my shot." He gestured at her with the digital camera in his hand.

She shrank down in her seat another inch, but still strained to catch Todd's eye. The choir fell silent. It was about to begin when he finally scanned her area.

She waved frantically, her heart throwing itself into its rhythm with the same joyful exuberance with which the first-grade choir had belted out their tunes.

She knew the moment her son recognized her, and her heart went still. Frozen.

Instead of the happiness she longed to see on his face when he realized she was there, his features pinched. His lips clamped shut and his eyes went narrow.

Mad.

His little hands clenched at his sides.

The crowd rustled restlessly in their seats, waiting for the play to begin. Todd had the first lines.

A teacher finally leaned over the edge of the stage and whispered something to him, probably thinking he'd forgotten his lines, but Todd's gaze never wavered from hers. It was as if he were sending her a message with a look.

You're not welcome here.

And her frozen heart shattered.

Ty watched Mia's expression change from one of motherly pride and the purest joy he'd ever seen to horror. Before he could ask what was wrong, Todd threw his top hat down and ran off the back of the stage, fumbling for a moment to find the break in the curtain.

Mia was after him before the crowd could gasp, and Ty was out of his seat and on her heels a heartbeat after that.

"Todd?" Mia called out backstage. "Todd, please!"

Both of them checked behind doors and down hallways, but there was no sign of the kid.

A bad feeling weighed on Ty's shoulders.

Mia ran down a corridor that led to the gymnasium. "Todd!" Her voice grew more frantic each time she called her son's name. She stopped at the intersection of two hallways, looking right.

Off to the left, Ty heard the slap of small footsteps, running. He tugged on the sleeve of Mia's shirt. "This way."

A door slammed, and they followed the sound to the boys' locker room. Mia charged through without even slowing down. The room smelled of bleach and socks, sweat and mildew.

It wasn't hard to find Todd. All they had to do was follow the sniffles.

Against the cold orange tile in a corner of the shower room, Mia's son huddled pitifully, his knees drawn up to his chest and his arms wrapped around his legs.

Mia went to him, but slowed when he visibly drew back and pressed his face tighter against his knees.

She crouched in front of him, not touching him, but her hand hovered in the air above his head. "Todd, baby, what's wrong?"

He lifted his head. His eyes were puffy and blood-shot. Tear tracks shone on his cheeks.

"Why did you come? You made me mess up in front of everybody."

"Todd, I came to see you. I wouldn't miss your—"

"You ruined it!" he shouted, practically spitting in his vehemence. "You ruined everything, just like you always do!"

Just as the kid finished, two more pairs of foot-steps padded across the shower floor. Ty glanced over his shoulder to see Citria and Nana Serrat. When Todd saw them, he scrambled to his feet, then, taking a wide berth around Mia, flung himself into his grandmother's arms.

Mia rose on wobbly legs. Pain carved deep grooves around her eyes. "I'm sorry."

Todd seemed not to hear her. "I wanna go home, Nana." He buried his cheek against her bosom. "Please. I wanna go home with you."

Nana Serrat kissed his forehead and stroked his hair. "It's all right, baby. I'll take you home."

Misty-eyed herself, the older woman gave Mia an apologetic look. When she turned to shuffle out of the locker room with Todd glued beneath her arm, Mia started to follow.

Ty held her back by the elbow.

"What are you doing?"

"Let him go, Mia."

"Let him go? He's upset. He needs me."

He tightened his grip on her arm when she tried

to pull away. "He needs some time to cool off, and to process the fact that you're back. You just surprised him is all."

"I thought he'd be happy to see me," she choked.

"He didn't know when you were coming home— probably had some doubts whether you would ever come back at all. We should have called and let him know we would be here."

Ty blasted himself mentally for not thinking of that two hours ago, and sighed. "He just wasn't ready. He was scared. Give him some time. He'll work it out."

"Oh, now you're Dr. Spock, too?"

"I know a thing or two about little boys that have been hurt by their mothers, yeah," he spat back just as sharply.

Mia didn't look convinced, but she quit struggling to get away.

"Let your mother-in-law take him home, put him to bed. I'll drive you when you're ready."

At the other end of the locker room, Citria opened the door for Nana, throwing a harsh look back over her shoulder at Mia.

If Ty ever had to describe a broken woman, the vision of Mia Serrat watching her son walk away from her, held under his grandmother's arm like a baby bird under a wing, would be an image that forever came to mind.

Chapter 8

Mia sat at the kitchen table with both hands wrapped around a full mug of green tea that had gone stone-cold, untouched. The chill of the porcelain leached into her veins, into her throat.

Todd's outburst played over and over in her mind like a recording on continuous loop. Her fingers trembled. She tightened her grip on the mug.

Nana appeared in the doorway wearing a blue flannel robe and slippers. "He finally cried himself to sleep," she said. The red rims around her eyes said she'd shed more than a few tears herself tonight.

"Thank you, Nana," Mia said.

Nana looked from Mia to the space behind her, where she knew Ty still stood, though he hadn't made a sound, or moved a muscle as far as Mia knew, in the last hour. "Good night, then."

"Good night."

Mia made no attempt to get up and take herself to bed. She doubted her legs would hold her.

"Good night," Ty added.

Nana ambled out of the kitchen looking a century older than she had just three days ago.

"It's late," Mia said without turning to her guest once her mother-in-law had gone. "What are you still doing here?"

"Waiting for you to offer me some tea," Ty deadpanned.

She unwrapped her stiff fingers from the ceramic and slid her mug down the table. He picked it up, set it in the microwave and set the oven for ninety seconds. When the timer dinged, he pulled the mug out and slid it back to her.

"I'll make my own, thanks."

He had a steaming mug in his hands by the time she worked up the courage to look at him. "So, having second thoughts about releasing me from custody?"

His lips pursed thoughtfully. "No."

"Liar. You'd be home in bed by now if you weren't."

He pulled up a chair and sat next to her. Their knees bumped as he scooted himself closer. "You're pretty upset."

"Ha!" The bitter laugh escaped before she could catch herself. "I think I have good reason."

"Yep," he agreed. "*That's* why I'm still here."

Once again she managed to hold back the tears that had been rising all night. "Just because I'm upset doesn't mean I'm thinking about hurting myself."

"Good."

A tremor started in her shoulders and radiated outward until her whole body shook. Her face crumpled. "My son said he hates me."

"Yeah, little bastard knew exactly which button to push, didn't he?"

Her back instantly stiffened. "Stop it! He's my son."

He held up his hands in surrender. "Just making a point. And getting mad is a lot better than getting all weepy, isn't it?"

She did feel stronger, all of a sudden. "I guess."

"Kids are a lot more tuned in to the adults around them than most people realize. They know our weak spots, and when they're hurting, they tend to lash out."

Mia sighed and sipped her reheated tea. "You really are Dr. Spock."

"Aw, come on. I'm a lot better looking than that old geezer."

Yes, he was. But she wasn't about to tell him that.

"So what do I do now? How do I get him back?"

"I don't think there is anything you can do to "get" him back. You have to wait for him to come to you. Just be there. He'll let you know when he's ready."

"*Just be there.* In other words, don't kill myself."

"Don't read more into my words than I meant."

She took another sip of tea and put the mug down. "Sorry. I'm still pretty raw tonight."

Todd's words still echoed in her head, though the accusations were quieter now. She suspected she'd be hearing his enraged cries in her head for a long, long time.

Todd wasn't the only one who needed some time to process.

She cleared her throat. "Not that you aren't welcome to camp out in my kitchen as long as you want to…but don't you have a home to go to?"

"Yeah, if you call a studio apartment full of secondhand furniture a home. Not that I'm there much anyway."

"Uncle Karl's working you like a dog, huh?"

"Dogs live like kings compared to me."

She smiled at that. He did a good puppy-dog face.

He walked toward the back door and she followed him. At the counter, he stopped, took a pen from the desk set by the phone and scribbled something on a message pad.

When he straightened to leave, she got choked up again. Maybe she didn't really want to be alone.

"Ty—Dr. Hansen—" she corrected, and took a deep breath. "Thank you."

The strength and warmth of his arms wrapping around her took her by surprise, as did the musky male smell.

It had been a long time since she'd smelled a man up close. She breathed deeply and let the scent of him fill her senses.

"You're welcome," he murmured in her ear, squeezing her gently.

He broke off the hug as suddenly as he'd initiated it, and crammed the note he'd scribbled on into her hand.

"What is it?" she asked, spreading the crumpled paper.

"My cell phone. Call me if you need me. Anytime."

Ty woke in the dark to an insistent chirping from his bedside table. His first thought was to throw his arm over there and kill whatever critter was making that racket.

His second was that he hoped he hadn't wrecked his cell phone playing Whac-A-Mole with it.

He finally got a firm hand on it and squinted to see the number on the caller ID. Making out the digits, a moment of panic punched him square in the gut.

He flipped the phone open. "Mia, are you all right?"

"I'm fine," she answered quietly. "Well…not fine, really. But okay, considering."

He glanced at the clock. "Then why are you calling me at 3:00 a.m.?"

"You said anytime."

He flopped back onto his pillow, his free hand flung out to his side. "Yes, I did."

"I'm sorry. I'll let you go back to sleep."

"No, wait." He *had* told her to call. Besides, there was something incredibly sexy about lying in the dark, naked under cool sheets with a woman who turned you on like no other whispering in your ear.

Her voice was low and husky, sleepy. He'd bet money she was lying in bed, too.

If he closed his eyes and laid the phone on the pillow, he could almost imagine she was here.

He scrubbed a hand over his face and tried to rally his thoughts. "I'm sorry. I'm just not a morning person."

"Or a middle-of-the-night person, apparently."

"Yeah. What's going on, Mia?"

"I was thinking about what you said."

"What did I say?"

"About having to wait for Todd to come to me. I think you're right. But if he won't talk to me, he still needs to talk to someone. He was so mad. He can't just keep that all bottled up inside. So I had an idea."

He waited for the other shoe to fall.

"As long as you're going to be seeing me—professionally I mean—you could see Todd, too."

"I don't think that's such a good idea, Mia. There are other doctors who specialize in kids."

"Not around here, there aren't."

Christ.

She was right, though. Based on what he'd seen tonight, the kid should be seeing someone, just to make sure he came through this okay.

"Has he seen someone in the past?"

"Yes. Nana had him work with a therapist after I tried… After I was hospitalized in California. But it was an older woman, and she said Todd didn't seem to care for her much. He misses his dad so much. He needs more than a doctor. He needs a man in his life. Someone he can talk guy stuff with."

Bam! There came that other shoe.

The problem was, once again she was probably right.

"I don't know if it will work. Right now the whole problem is that he's mad at you. Once he knows I'm your doctor, too, he'll most likely be just as mad at me by association."

"It's worth a try, though, isn't it? We have to try something."

He threw a wrist over his eyes. "Yeah, we do."

Even if it inevitably brought him even closer to Mia Serrat.

What the hell. He was going to be seeing her regularly anyhow. In for a penny, in for a pound.

In a week's time, Ty had settled into a comfortable routine in the Serrat household. He had driven over three times in the evenings for sessions with Mia. At least they called them sessions. Honestly, the woman just didn't need his doctorly skills. She was worried about her son, sure, but she was coping. There hadn't been any hint of further lapses in her contact with reality.

Following the routine they'd started at the hospital, they usually walked as they talked. After about ten minutes, the "therapy" generally drifted toward more popular concerns—movies, music, books. Their tastes varied wildly. He tended toward

The Simpsons while she favored *Seinfeld* reruns. He liked country, she listened to alternative rock. He read mostly textbooks, while she devoured thrillers.

Come to think of it, he really should discourage that particular reading choice for her.

The one thing they had in common was that they made each other smile. Sometimes, he even managed to make her laugh. It was getting easier being around her. There was something to be said for being able to spend time with a woman he liked without the yoke of a relationship hanging around his neck.

She was his patient. There could never be anything more than friendship between them, so there was no pressure.

Unfortunately there was also no touching, kissing or sex but hey, a guy couldn't have everything, could he?

After their walks Mia would make a point of inviting him to dinner, and at a convenient point after the meal, find an excuse to slip away, leaving him with Todd.

So far, the kid was skittish as a wild horse. As soon as Ty got too close, he ran away. Tonight held a glimmer of promise, though. Todd's favorite TV show was on, and Ty had planted himself directly in front of the only television in the house. Nana and Mia had made themselves scarce.

"You really like this stuff?" Ty nodded toward the TV set just as Homer Simpson let out a loud "Doh!"

Todd shrugged. "It's okay. You can change the channel if you want."

"No, that's okay."

Todd picked at the arm of his chair. "You don't have to pretend to want to watch TV with me, you know. I know what you are. A psychiatrist."

Sharp kid. Takes after his mother.

"You've seen psychiatrists before, haven't you?"

He made a face. "Dr. Sandstrom. She was boring. Are you my mom's psychiatrist?"

"Yep."

"So how come you're always over here, like eating dinner and stuff?"

"I like it here." He rubbed his belly. "Your mom's a good cook."

"When she's here," Todd muttered.

Ty shrugged. Neither one of them was ready to go down that path yet. "So what was wrong with Dr. Sandstrom that made her boring?"

"She always just wanted to talk and stuff. Or get me to draw pictures." He screwed up his face. "With crayons, like a little kid!"

"Yeah, I can see how that would get old. What do you like to do if you don't like to draw?"

"Play video games."

"Awesome. Me, too. What've you got?"

"Lots of things. *Land of Legends* is my favorite. I kick butt at that one. My high score is over two million."

"No way!"

"Uh-huh." He looked skeptically at Ty and Ty held his breath.

"Wanna see?" Todd asked.

"You bet." He breathed, a weight off his chest. He had the kid hooked. Now all he had to do was reel him in.

Mia listened to the sounds of rockets exploding, missiles whistling through the air and bone-crunching collisions coming from Todd's room until she could barely contain herself. Ty and Todd were playing, and from the sound of it, were engaged in full-scale, no-holds-barred warfare punctuated by the occasional gleeful "Gotcha!" or moan of defeat. Or childish laugh.

She'd never heard anything so beautiful.

When Ty finally emerged, she cornered him on the front porch. "So? How'd it go?"

"Great. I scored 1,737,292. Unfortunately, Todd scored 1,899,267." He shook his head. "Damn, the kid is good."

She made an exasperated sound and crossed her arms over her chest. "I wasn't asking who won the war."

He started down the steps toward his car. "We played video games, Mia, that's it. It's going to take time. If I pressure him for more now, I'll scare him off. Be patient."

She chewed on her lip. "Patience has never been my strong suit."

He rolled his head around to look at her as he unlocked the door to his Volkswagen. "I never would have guessed."

"Maybe I know a way to speed things up. One of Todd's favorite things to do with his dad when we came to visit here in the wintertime was to go sledding. Maybe if you're not busy this weekend, we could head out to the park on Mayborne Road. The one with the big hill."

He folded his body up into the tiny car. "I'll have to see if I can get away from the hospital."

She winked at him. "I have some pull with the director. Seriously, I don't think Todd will go if it's just me and him, but if you ask him…"

"I'll try," he conceded. To tell the truth, she'd had him at sledding. Her body snuggled up tight against him, his arms and legs wrapped around hers. What was not to like?

Chapter 9

Ty stopped by the hospital early Saturday morning to drop off some notes for Dr. Raymond, who was covering his shift so Ty could make his sledding date. He instantly regretted the decision. On top of the stack of files and forms in his mail slot was a pink message slip with a terse message to check in with Dr. Serrat as soon as he arrived.

Crap. What was the Kaiser doing in on a Saturday anyway?

He trudged upstairs. The director stood at a bay window looking out at the landscape as if he'd been waiting on him.

"Do you know a sheriff's deputy named Campbell?"

"Chuck? Sure, why?"

"Do you know why he would be making inquiries into my family's business?" He sounded like he was talking without opening his lips. No doubt the old man was pissed.

"Not really."

"Then let me fill you in. He said he was investigating a possible attempted murder. On Mia Serrat. Do you have any idea how he might have gotten the idea that my niece's incidents were anything other than paranoid delusions?"

"Ah, I asked him to come and talk to Mia when she was here. I thought it might help her to—"

"He was asking questions about Mia's financial status," the Kaiser cut in, leaning forward across his desk. "His implications were clear."

As were Uncle Karl's. The menace in his glare was unmistakable. *Don't mess with the Serrat family.*

Ty swallowed hard. "I—I'm sure Deputy Campbell's questions were just routine."

Karl's chair creaked as he sat back, appraised Ty. A sweat popped on the back of Ty's neck, but he didn't flinch under the old man's scrutiny.

"Actually the deputy was quite correct in his concern," Karl said.

Ty blinked. "He was?"

"Sam Serrat was quite the entrepreneur. He made a small fortune doing computer graphics and animation in California. He did work for Spielberg, Scorsese…all the big names. Of course Mia inherited all that money when Sam died."

"And if something happened to Mia?" Ty asked, intrigued, and yet wary of the direction this conversation had taken.

"Everything would be held in trust for Todd."

Ty's thoughts circled around that, not sure what to make of it until Karl continued.

"And just to be sure we understand each other on this matter, you should know that I am named in Mia's will to manage the trust for the boy, should anything happen to her."

Ty's thoughts quit circling and fell flat into the pit of his stomach.

Crap.

Karl enunciated pointedly. His blue eyes sat like chips of ice in the hollows of his weathered face. "Do you think I would kill my niece-in-law to get control of her money? Do you think I would steal that money from my own grand-nephew, just a *boy?*"

Ty lowered his gaze. "No. Of course not."

Silence sat between them for a long moment.

"Then in the future, I'd appreciate it if you'd restrict your treatment plans to the confines of medicine, Doctor."

The warning in the director's tone set Ty back. He took a deep breath and dropped the defense he had been about to shoot back. "Yes, sir. I'll talk to Deputy Campbell."

"See that you do."

The Kaiser seemed momentarily appeased. Ty stood to leave, but before he made his escape Dr.

Serrat stopped him. "How is Mia by the way?" His tone had softened from harsh to merely gruff.

"She's doing well."

"I understand you're seeing Todd now, too."

"Just informally. Mia was worried about him, asked me to get a read on how he's handling all this."

Karl Serrat scratched his chin. "Yes, that's probably a good idea. But I understand you're taking them sledding this morning. Do you think that's wise?"

"Actually they're taking me. Both of them have negative histories with mental-health professionals. I seem to get more accomplished with them outside of the clinical setting."

Karl considered, then spoke, his voice cold. "Just be careful, Doctor. An ethics inquiry at this juncture in your career could severely limit your future in the medical profession."

Message received, director. One more trip wire in the minefield. The warning was clear. *Stay the hell away from my niece.* "Thanks for the reminder."

He stopped by his office long enough to call Chuck, but got voice mail, then took off. He'd have to hurry to make it to Eternal in time to meet Mia and Todd.

He needn't have worried. They were fifteen minutes late. By the time they arrived at the sledding hill—he'd figured meeting them there made it look like more of an appointment and less of a date than driving together—Todd was already ruddy-cheeked and breathless.

The boy high-fived him enthusiastically when he

bounced out of his mom's SUV covered from head to toe in winter wear.

"All set, kiddo?" he laughed.

"This is going to be so cool." Todd could hardly stand still while Ty pulled out the sled. Seconds later, the kid was pulling him up the hill, then he was zooming down the slope on an old-fashioned wooden sled with twin runners, trying to steer with his feet and hold one wriggling, squealing boy on with his arms.

Snow whipped into his eyes and down his shirt. His gloves became ice mitts. His toes were numb, and he was loving every minute of it. This outing, and the dinners at the Serrat house, were supposed to be about Mia and Todd, but he was getting as much out of the meetings as they were. Every day, every hour, he spent out of the hospital, out from under Karl Serrat's heavy watch, the tension slipped away from him. Weight was lifted from his shoulders and he found himself smiling more, even laughing.

Especially today. Each trip down the hill they averted near disaster and Ty arrived at a safe stop laughing and sputtering only to be dragged back to the starting point by Todd.

After about the sixth trip, Ty was huffing. Todd wasn't even winded.

Ty looked back up the hill at Mia, standing at the top and stomping her feet. "How about you and your mom go this time? I'll take a little break and try out that hot chocolate she brought for us."

Todd kicked at the snow. "Maybe I'll have some chocolate, too."

"Don't worry, I'll save you some. Come on, your mom hasn't had a turn." Ty figured this was as good a time as any. "You still mad at her?"

The kid shrugged.

"Hey, that whole thing with the hospital was my fault, you know."

Todd looked up at him suspiciously.

"She could've been hurt falling down that hill, and I was worried about her. I conned her into staying for a few days. Just so I could make sure she was okay." Pretending his boot laces needed retying, he bent down to Todd's level. "I mean, you'd want to make sure she was okay, too, right?"

"I guess."

He straightened up. "Turns out she's fine, so why don't you go take a ride down the hill with her?"

The look of pure longing on Todd's face as he stared up the hill at his mom was enough to tug at the strings of the toughest heart. He was close, so close.

But not quite ready yet. "Nah," he said.

"All right," Ty said, and took the rope to the sled from Todd's hand and started up the hill. "You don't want to ride with her, I will."

Mia smiled as she watched her son and Ty march back up the hill covered in white powder. "You want some chocolate now?" she offered when they reached the top.

"Nope." Ty took the thermos from her out-stretched hand and gave it to Todd. "It's your turn."

"Oh, no. I'm not going down the hill on that contraption." She started to back up. "You boys just keep—"

Ty grabbed her around the waist and swung her toward the sled. "Shh," he said, and cut a look toward a perplexed-looking Todd. "Sit."

She did as she was told, still trying to figure out what Ty was up to, but understanding from his look that now was not the time to ask.

She settled onto the front of the sled and Ty lowered his long body into place behind her. His arms wrapped securely around her waist and the insides of his legs brushed the outside of hers, keeping all her limbs aboard. All in all, the sensation was quite pleasant, even if she shouldn't have noticed.

"You ready?" His breath tickled her cheek.

"Not really." The hill looked a lot longer and a whole lot steeper when one was sitting on a rocket ship on skids.

"Good." Ty laughed, and took a moment to give Todd a long look. He pulled Mia's body snug against his. Out of the corner of her eye, Mia saw Todd frown and knew he hadn't missed the motion.

This did not seem like a Dr. Spock–approved tech-nique.

"Save us some hot chocolate," he told her son, then shoved off. "We'll need it after a couple of spins."

"A couple?" Todd complained, but Ty pretended not to hear.

She quit puzzling what the good doctor was up to when the rush of wind hit her face. The speed quickly became dizzying. They were flying! The snow stung her cheeks and forced her to narrow her eyes to slits.

The sled bucked beneath her, threatening to unseat her. It fishtailed left, then right, but Ty countered every move, holding her tight against him and using their weight as one to keep them on a straight track until the very bottom when the sled curved sharply right as they slowed and rolled them both into a drift.

She came up with a mouthful of snow and Ty laughed at her. She scooped a mitten full of the white stuff into his face, and he retaliated with a snowball to her back when she made the mistake of turning away from him.

Something broke open inside Mia, and she realized this last year, sitting in her room writing in her journal and counting days, this life she'd so treasured, wasn't living at all.

This was living. Speeding down a hill and snowball-fighting and your face heating at the expression on a man's face when he looked at you a certain way. That was living.

The realization took her breath away. "Come on," she said. "Let's do it again."

"Love to," Ty answered and quirked his mouth up in an ironic smile. His gaze moved up the hill and hers followed. "But I think someone else wants a turn."

Above them, Todd was waving impatiently for them to return. Twenty feet before she reached the top, he called down to her. "Come on, Mom, hurry up. It's our turn!"

She turned to Ty in excitement, and he winked at her.

"How did you do it?" she whispered.

"Easy," he answered just before they reached the top. "I appealed to one of the primary male motivators. Jealousy."

The rest of her morning belonged exclusively to Todd. She sledded with him, built a snowman with him, made snow angels beside him, and loved him with all her heart.

Every now and then she found a second to sneak a grateful smile to Ty, who stood by, serving up hot chocolate and dry mittens on demand.

When they split up in the parking lot to go their separate ways just before lunchtime, she mouthed *thank you* to him before he turned away. She wished she had more to give him. It hardly seemed a fair exchange. He'd given her her son back, and all she had in return was words.

By the time Mia had made the thirty-minute drive back to Nana's house, she was so tired she could hardly keep her eyes open, but it was a happy tired. The kind brought on by fresh air and laughter. Not to mention twelve or fourteen climbs up a sixty-foot hill covered in snow and dragging a sled. Maybe she could get in a nap after she made a bowl of hot soup for Todd.

"I wonder where Nana is?" Her mother-in-law's car wasn't in the drive.

Mia used the electric door-opener to raise the garage door, then pulled inside. As soon as she turned the engine off, Todd scampered out his door.

"Go see if she left a note," she told him. "While I unload the car." She wanted to get the wet boots, scarves and gloves laid out to dry before they mildewed, and the empty hot chocolate thermos was rolling around the floorboards somewhere.

Todd stomped through the door into the house calling for his Nana. Mia hit the button to close the garage door.

She heard footsteps back on the step to the door into the house and assumed it was Todd back already. "No note?" she asked without turning.

She never got an answer. Instead an arm closed around her throat. Another, this one holding a foul-smelling rag, clamped over her mouth. Mia tried to scream, but couldn't make a sound.

God, Todd was in the house. She had to protect her son.

She tried to stomp down on her assailant's instep, but he was too quick. She tried to bite his hand, gouge his eyes, anything, but he had taken her by surprise. His grip on her was too secure.

Spots danced before her eyes. Her field of vision narrowed to a tunnel and blurred. A sad sense of irony bubbled inside her. Just two short years ago she would have welcomed death. Her battle against the pain that had festered inside her had been long and hard fought, and now that she'd won it, now that she wanted to live, someone else's hand would accomplish what hers had not.

He was going to kill her—of that much she was sure—yet despite the fact that the future she'd worked so hard to secure for herself was being stolen, her last conscious thought was not for herself. It was for her son.

Todd was in the house, hopefully unaware of what was happening so nearby. Please let him stay where he was. Please don't let him decide to come see what was taking her so long.

It didn't matter what they did to her, but dear God, whoever was doing this, please don't let them hurt Todd.

Despite the fact that his mind kept wandering to a steep white slope of snow, a towheaded boy and the mother who looked at him as though he was joy incarnate, Ty managed to make quick work of his patient chart updates. All except one.

He kicked back in the chair in his tiny office and laced his fingers behind his head, staring at Mia's folder as if it were a snake coiled to strike. It wasn't a bad comparison, actually, since he had a sinking feeling his relationship with Mia was going to bite him in the ass if he got in any deeper with her.

This morning's sledding trip hadn't just been the kind of day he'd dreamed about—and never gotten—

when he was Todd's age. It had been the kind of day he hadn't let himself dream about as a grown man. He'd been too focused on his work to be distracted by women. But Mia, standing at the top of the hill and smiling at him as though he were her white knight, eyes so warm he was surprised the snow hadn't melted on the spot, handing him a steaming mug of hot chocolate, laughing and gasping, their bodies pressed together as they'd sped down the hill together, had made him realize exactly what he'd been missing. Now that he'd had a taste of what he'd been denying himself, he wanted more. And he wanted it with Mia.

He drummed his fingers on her chart. Leave it to him to get hung up on the one woman he couldn't have.

Maybe that was why he was so attracted to her. He could flirt with the idea of a relationship, knowing he could never actually act on the idea. It was safe.

And now he was psychoanalyzing himself. Not good.

Picking up his pen, he opened Mia's folder, noted his conclusions and scribbled a note to close the case, recommend an occasional checkup with another doctor in the future. She was going to be fine. Todd was going to be fine. There was no reason for him to continue seeing them in an official capacity.

No reason for him to continue seeing them in any capacity at all. It wasn't just the wrath of Karl Serrat he feared. Dating a former patient was still an ethical gray area, and truth be told, he just couldn't afford the distraction right now.

He would call Mia and tell her, give her some names of reputable doctors, but he couldn't see her, personally or professionally, again.

Resolved to get it over with as soon as possible, he stood, shrugged into his coat and slung the stack of case files under one arm and insurance forms under the other. He dumped the case files in Director Serrat's inbox for review and approval, then headed for the door. He wanted to make the call where he was sure there wouldn't be other ears listening in.

As he stepped into the bitter December wind and flipped his phone open, another call came in. The caller ID read Chuck Campbell.

Belatedly he remembered the Kaiser's morning order to put a halt to the deputy's investigation into the Serrat family and the voice mail he'd left Chuck.

Ty pressed the talk button. "Hey, man, it's about time you called me back."

"Ty, where are you?"

His old friend's voice was low and tight, raising the hairs on the back of Ty's neck. Sirens wailed in the background.

"At the hospital. Where are you?"

"At the Serrat house. I got a situation here."

The wind kicked up, clawing inside Ty's coat and trailing icy fingers down his back.

"Looks like your girlfriend tried to off herself

again," Chuck continued. "And this time she just might have succeeded."

Ty's heart skipped a beat. "There's gotta be some mistake."

"Uh-uh," Chuck grunted.

Could the situation get any worse?

Chapter 10

Mia woke with a start, gasping, choking. She clawed at her chest, at the great weight there, at her face. She couldn't breathe. Her hand hit something over her mouth, knocked it aside.

She writhed, desperate for air. Her tongue was so thick she couldn't breathe around it and her mouth felt as if someone had stuffed it with cotton while she slept.

She tried to sit, found herself too weak. All she could do was cough. Her lungs were on fire!

"She's coming around," a disembodied voice said from her side. "Page Dr. Smith."

Mia pried her eyelids open far enough to see the woman who had spoken, a short round woman in a white dress. A nurse? She must be in the hospital, then.

She coughed again and the nurse shifted the oxygen mask she'd knocked aside back over her mouth.

Suddenly Mia remembered. The garage. The man. The rag over her mouth, the feeling of being suffocated.

She tried to talk and gagged on her tongue.

"Quiet now, Ms. Serrat. Just relax, you're going to be fine." The woman patted her on the shoulder unconvincingly. At least she was able to scrape in a raw breath of the cool gas flowing through the mask.

Two men she hadn't seen across the room stepped up to her bedside. One wore the uniform of a sheriff's deputy. The other was in plain clothes, but a leather-backed shield was clipped to his belt.

"Ms. Serrat," the man she guessed to be a detective said. "Can you tell us what happened this afternoon?"

Words were like acid on her raw throat. "I don't… Someone grabbed—" She fell into a fit of coughing.

"Someone grabbed…you? Someone grabbed you?"

She managed a nod, her eyes tearing.

"Who grabbed you?"

"Don't…know. What…happened?"

"You don't remember what happened?"

She shook her head.

"Your mother-in-law found you in the garage with your car running. You had stuffed rags under the doors to keep the exhaust from escaping." The two police officers looked somberly at each other, then at her. "You tried to kill yourself, and you almost succeeded."

This time she managed to raise herself a few

inches off the bed, shaking her head roughly before crashing back to the pillow. "No," she croaked. "No."

The deputy rolled the flat brim of his hat around in his hands. The detective cleared his throat. "Ms. Serrat, I'm aware of the claims you made recently that someone was trying to kill—"

"Not claims! Someone—" Cough.

"Ms. Serrat…"

"Someone tried—" Cough. Cough. No. She didn't try to kill herself. They had to believe her!

"Ms. Serrat, we can talk about that later. What we really need to know right now is where your son is."

Her body went still. Even her heart stopped beating. "Todd?"

"Yes, your son Todd. Where is he?"

"He's…he's home." She coughed and sputtered, managed to control the spasm this time. "He's in the house!"

"No, ma'am. He's not."

The stillness was broken by violent shaking. She threw herself upright and swung her legs over the side of the bed. Her gown gaped open and she didn't care. She had to find her son.

The two officers grabbed her by the upper arms before her bare feet hit the floor. She pushed and pulled against them, only to have them tighten their grip.

"Please. Let me go." She sagged backward, then surged forward to no avail. "I have to find my son."

"Ma'am, just tell us what you did with him, and we'll find him."

"What *I* did?" Her eyes felt too large for her face. "You think I—?" She lunged forward, and one of her clenched fists clipped the detective in the jaw.

"All right! That's enough." The detective grabbed her with both hands and wrestled her back to the bed. She squirmed and kicked, trying to find the air to scream while both men held her down.

"What the *hell?*" A familiar voice boomed from the doorway.

Mia nearly cried in relief.

In two strides Ty was across the room and had the detective by the collar, hauling him backward. The deputy, looking sheepish, took a step back of his own accord.

The detective struggled out of Ty's grasp. "Back off, Doctor."

Ty's pulse pounded in his ears. "You back off. Back all the way the hell out of this room off. Right now!"

The detective straightened his collar. "I'm questioning a—"

"Nobody's questioning anybody until she's been cleared medically."

"That's not your call."

"No, but it is mine." A fourth man had quietly joined the standoff, a stethoscope hanging around his neck. *Dr. Smith,* the name sewn over the breast pocket of his white coat read. "Now I'd appreciate it if you'd all get out of my emergency room. That includes you, Dr. Hansen."

Ty looked ready to argue, but instead took a deep breath and turned to Mia. "I'll be right outside."

"No." Her voice sounded like the churn of rocks in a tumbler. Already Dr. Smith was herding the men out of the room. "You have to go to Nana's. You have to look for—" She couldn't hold back another cough. As Ty was backed out the door, she managed to finish. "You have to find Todd. Please. Find Todd."

The door had no sooner swung shut behind him than Ty spun on Chuck. "What the hell is she talking about?"

From Chuck's expression, Ty knew the news wouldn't be good. Chuck was known as an easygoing guy. He didn't take himself or anyone else too seriously, but there was no trace of laughter in his eyes now. No hint of a smile on his face.

"Mrs. Serrat found Mia in the garage, like I told you, but she couldn't find Todd. He's missing."

Ty swore—one of the really bad words he rarely used—and raked a hand through his hair. His mind raced.

"Did you check the house real good? Maybe he got scared and he's hiding."

"He's not in the house."

"What about outside? He's only eight years old. He couldn't have gotten far, for Christ's sake."

"We've set up a command post at the house. We've got teams coming in to search. If he's wandering around out there, we'll find him."

Ty caught Chuck's sideways glance. He'd known him long enough to read his body language. "What do you mean 'if'?"

Chuck turned his hat around and around in his hands. "There was no sign Todd was in the house when Mia tried…when she locked herself in the garage. We didn't find his coat or his boots."

"Because he's wearing them."

"Maybe. Or maybe he never made it home from the sledding trip."

Ty's blood ran cold as he realized what the deputy was thinking. "No. She wouldn't hurt him. She loves that kid."

"Loves him enough to want to take him with her when she goes? We've seen it before. A mother who hurts her kid—even a kid she loves."

Yeah, he'd seen it up close and personal. But not Mia.

"I don't believe it."

"Believe me, buddy, I hope I'm wrong. But her little boy is missing, and until we have something else to go on, Mia is our prime suspect."

Ty sat in a hard plastic chair in the Eternal Emergency Care Clinic waiting room, his elbows on his knees and his head in his hands. In his mind, every moment of this morning's sledding trip played on continuous loop as he analyzed every word she'd said, every expression, looking for something that forecast the events that had followed.

He just didn't see it. He didn't see her as a murder-suicide about to happen.

But then, did anyone ever see it? That was the horror of mental illness—it hid behind many masks.

He scrubbed his face, the loop starting over with Todd waving from the backseat as her car pulled into the park, but before he got any further, the sound of hushed voices entering the waiting area had him looking up. His gut tightened. Nana, Citria and Karl Serrat, all with equally grave expressions, took seats on the couches across the room. Nana sniffed and dabbed at her eyes with a wadded tissue. Citria held her hand.

Ty rose stiffly and walked over to them, his fingertips jammed in the pockets of his jeans.

"You." Nana sniffed again and wiped the tip of her nose. "You said she was all right. You said she was well."

"I'm sorry, Mrs. Serrat—"

Karl's eyes glared up, squeezing his sister's hand. "There'll be a full case review as soon as I get back in the office. If I find your actions in this matter negligent in any way, you'll be more than sorry, Doctor."

Ty held the director's gaze through the tirade, forced his attention back to Nana. His instinct was to defend himself, but that was a discussion for a different time, a different place.

"Mrs. Serrat, can you tell me what happened?" he asked gently.

"I—I told the police. I just went out for some red

beans and hamburger meat. It's getting so cold, I was going to make a big pot of chili."

She looked up and Ty nodded, encouraging her to continue.

"When I came home, the garage door was closed. I thought Mia wasn't home yet, until I opened it and I found her…I found her inside." The tears ran freely down Nana's face now.

"And Todd wasn't there?"

She shook her head. "After I called 911, I realized he wasn't in the house. I ran outside yelling for him, looking everywhere, but there was no sign of him."

"So you never saw him after they left to go sledding this morning?"

She inhaled a stuttering breath, on the brink of an all-out cry.

Karl gave him a look of warning. "That's enough, Dr. Hansen. Don't you think my sister has been through enough?"

"I'm just trying to understand what happened."

Citria spoke up. "My sister-in-law tried to kill herself. That's what happened. And she probably slaughtered my nephew—all we had left of my poor brother—before she did."

Ty's fists clenched at Citria's insensitive choice of words, but he held his temper in check. "That's not what Mia says happened."

Citria laughed bitterly. "Mia is crazy, Doc. Don't you get that yet? She's a Looney Tune, and this is all your fault. You should have kept her locked up when you had her. This time when we put her away, we're going to get someone to do it who will lock her up for good and throw away the key."

Ty looked from Serrat to Serrat, waiting for Nana or Karl to dispute Citria's claim, to offer even a glimmer of sympathy for Mia, but it never came.

Mia had lost another family, and with it what little support structure she had left in her life.

Mia woke to a room nearly dark, lit only by a small light above the door, and a dark shadow looming over her. She gasped and threw her arms up reflexively.

"Mia, shh. It's me."

Her heart thundered against her ribs. "Ty?"

"Yeah."

She sank back into the mattress. "What are you doing sitting in the dark?"

"I'm not supposed to be here. Your family forbade me to see you. I had to wait until most of the staff was gone and sneak in."

Sleep still fogged her brain. "My family? Nana? Why—?"

Realization finally sank in. "Oh, God. They think I—"

"It's all right."

"No, no it's not. They think I hurt Todd, and they blame you. Is there any word?" Her voice rose in pitch, as she suddenly wondered if Ty was there to break bad news to her. "Have they found him?"

"No." His low voice was soothing. "They're still looking. Everyone is still looking."

She breathed a little easier. "They're going to have me committed again, aren't they? They're going to take me back to MHMH."

"Not just yet. Dr. Smith is keeping you here for a few days. Your body chemistry is all screwed up from the carbon dioxide, and you need regular oxygen therapy or your lungs could be damaged permanently."

"A few days." She felt as if she'd just been diagnosed with a terminal illness and had only a few days left to live. "We have to find Todd."

"You have to stay here. Don't even think about walking out. Karl insisted on a security guard at your door. Cost me fifty bucks to get ten minutes in here."

She tugged at his sleeve. "Then you have to find Todd for me. Please."

"Can you think of any place special he likes? Kids like to go places they feel safe when they're scared."

"He plays down by the creek a lot. Oh, God. It's starting to ice over. What if he fell through…"

"Easy. If he's out there, more than likely it's because he's scared, not because he's hurt."

"It's going to be so cold tonight. He can't stay out there. You've got to find him. Please."

"I'll try, Mia." A rap sounded on the door. "My time is up. I've got to go. I just wanted you to know I was here for you. Even if I can't be here, in this room, for you. Don't give up, Mia."

She wanted to tell him she wouldn't, but to be

honest, she couldn't be sure. If something had happened to Todd…

She stopped him at the door with a word. "Ty…do you believe me?"

His face was cast half in shadow, half in light from the little lamp above him.

"I'm trying, Mia," he said. "I'm trying."

Chapter 11

"Ty, man, we've got to get back to the command post. I can't feel anything from the knees down."

"Yeah, me, either, and we've been out here what…two hours? Think what the kid must feel like if he's been out here all night."

"You know as well as I do that if the kid is out here, he's long past feeling anything. I don't care how scared or pissed off at his mother he is. No one would stay out in this weather if they were able to get in."

"I'm not convinced she did it, Chuck."

"Jesus, what do you want, a video replay?"

"That would help. Come on, even you had some doubts."

"After the first attempt, sure. After the second,

not so much, but I was willing to go with it for your sake."

"You were investigating the Serrats. Did you find anything?"

"Other than that they're a little strange and a lot private, no. You know the old man gets control of the money if Mia dies?"

"Yeah, I know. But he's just the trustee, not the beneficiary. So if Mia and Todd were out of the picture, who would get the money?"

"Nana. You're not telling me you think that old lady could do this?"

Ty shrugged. "Maybe."

Chuck threw his hands up. The beam of his flashlight bounced around the naked tree limbs overhead. "Then what are you telling me?"

Ty stopped to catch his breath. "Hell if I know."

"Then let's try something simpler. Why are we on a beeline for the creek?"

"Because I said I wasn't convinced Mia did it. Not that it wasn't possible, and Mia said he likes to play down there."

"You don't think he's out playing. Or hiding."

"No." Ty hated that his thoughts had even turned in this direction. Hated more to put words to them, give them credence. "Look, sometimes good people who commit horrendous crimes, especially against people they love, want to be caught and punished. They just can't come out and say it."

It only took Chuck a couple of seconds to catch

on. "Son of a— You think she told you where the body is. In her own way."

He swallowed the lump in his throat. "God, I hope not."

By dawn, exhaustion and frostbite had forced Ty and Chuck back to the command post. They stood huddled under a canvas shelter with steaming cups of coffee, watching the canine teams brief. After their fruitless trek up and down the banks of the creek in the dark, Chuck had called on a local volunteer search team.

The black Lab, he was told, was a "live find" dog—trained to search for any living human in a given area. The two German shepherds were human-remains-detection dogs. Cadaver dogs, their purpose obvious and unthinkable.

The coffee didn't sit well on Ty's empty stomach, and he threw the half-full cup in the trash. "I'm going to catch an hour's sleep in my car," he told Chuck. "Then I'm going back out."

When he woke to the sound of barking dogs, nearly three hours had passed. He hurried out of his car as the canine teams shuffled in, stiff from the cold. One of the handlers looked up at him as he walked by and shook his head.

Ty let out the breath he'd been holding. They hadn't found anything.

Mia stifled another cough while she waited for the cameraman to adjust the lights and the reporter to freshen up her lipstick and primp her hair in the lobby of the Eternal Emergency Care Clinic. She'd asked for this opportunity to go on television, and the news channel had jumped at the chance for an interview. Word of the missing eight-year-old in Massachusetts was making headlines across the Northeast, and would probably be picked up by the national wires by evening.

The cameraman motioned for quiet. "Four, three, two, one." Then he pointed at the reporter, Marika Towne.

After a brief introduction from the anchor in the studio, which only Marika could hear in her earpiece, the reporter turned to Mia, who sat in her wheelchair on a raised platform.

"Ms. Serrat, tell us about your son." She smiled as if she were interviewing the proud mom of a boy who'd just caught the game-winning touchdown for his team.

Mia held up a picture, willing back her tears. "His name is Todd. Samuel Todd Serrat. He's four foot one, ninety pounds and has sandy-blond hair and a few freckles on his nose."

"And he's been missing since yesterday?" Again, the too-bright smile.

"Yes, yesterday, early afternoon, after we returned home from sledding."

"You believe someone took Todd by force?"

"Yes, he wouldn't have left otherwise. Someone had to have taken him." She bit her trembling lip and looked straight into the camera. She managed to get the words out, but she couldn't stop a couple of tears from spilling onto her cheeks. "Please, whoever has him, let him go. Whatever you want, whatever you need, just tell me. Just let him come home."

"Folks, the number of the sheriff's department is on the bottom of your screen now. Please call if you have any information on this missing child. Thank you, Mia, and God bless."

That was it? "Wait—" She wanted to ask the community to help. To beg her friends and neighbors to look out for a little boy. She wanted to offer money. She wanted to plead.

Marika angled away from her. "That's it, Steve, a passionate plea from the mother of the missing eight-year-old right here in Eternal."

The nurse behind Mia's chair swept her away, but on the monitor in the waiting room, Mia caught the last bit of the interview as she rolled past.

"—true the mother may be behind this disappearance herself?" the anchor asked from the newsroom.

Marika's eyes danced on the screen, clearly happy to dish out this juicy tidbit. "Yes, it's a tragic story, Steve, but police believe Ms. Serrat may be behind her son's disappearance, as part of an apparent murder-suicide attempt that failed. At least the suicide part. Unfortunately it may already be too late to help this beautiful little boy."

Bands of anger tightened around Mia's chest.

No.

Her fists clenched on the arms of the chair. Now

no one would believe her. No one would look for Todd. They would just cluck their tongues over the "poor child" and go back to their Sunday suppers without a second thought.

Ty caught Mia's interview on the portable TV a cashier had tucked behind the cash register at the Quickway gas and convenience store. He paid cash for the gas he'd put in his VW and the thick coffee he'd poured from the self-serve carafe at the back of the store. If the brew tasted as bitter as it smelled, it was likely to eat through his stomach, but he needed the caffeine and the warmth after a long night of fruitless searching for Mia's missing son.

The ordeal was taking a toll on her. He could see it in her eyes, which had lost their light, the creases on her forehead, the bloodless complexion of her cheeks. Yet her back was straight in the wheelchair, her shoulders square. Her voice trembled with the terror of a mother afraid for her child.

That kind of emotion couldn't be faked. Whether anyone else believed her or not, Mia Serrat was convinced she had not hurt her son.

She made a good impression, he thought. Won some people over to her side. At least until the smarmy reporter closed out the interview with her own suppositions. Judge, jury and executioner, all rolled into one, she condemned Mia with a smile on her face and an eager gleam into the lens of the camera. The whole scenario reminded Ty of the old song "Dirty Laundry."

The only story bigger than a missing eight-year-old boy was a missing eight-year-old boy whose own mother was responsible for his disappearance, and that was the story Marika Towne reported, whether there was any evidence of its truth or not.

Wondering if Mia had heard the end of the report, Ty flicked open his cell phone. Mia's family had blocked him from seeing her at the hospital. He could only hope they hadn't thought to stop her calls, as well.

She picked up on the third ring, her voice tentative. "Hello?"

"Mia, it's Ty."

He heard her expel a breath. "Oh, I thought it was another reporter. The phone's been ringing off the hook, but I didn't dare not answer it, in case there was some news— Oh, God, are you calling about Todd? Have they found something?"

"No," he reassured her, if telling a mother that her son was still missing could be considered reassurance. "Nothing yet." And there likely wouldn't be, as the searchers had packed up and left Nana Serrat's house.

Not wanting to break the news that the search had been called off, he changed the subject. "How are you feeling?"

"Better. It's easier to breathe now, and my head is clearer."

"Have you remembered anything else? Anything at all?"

"No, it's all still a jumble. I just remember feeling

something—someone—behind me, and then a funny smell and something over my mouth. Then it's all black until I woke up here. I've tried." The pitch of her voice rose in desperation. "I just can't remember anything else."

"It's all right." Ty rolled his head around to release some tension. It had been a long night. It looked like it was going to be a long day, as well. "We'll find him some other way."

"God, they took him, didn't they? Whoever attacked me had to have taken him. I was hoping—this is a terrible thing to hope—but I was hoping he had just seen something. Seen whoever tried to kill me, or seen me in the garage and thought... I was hoping he'd just gotten scared and run away. But he'd have come back by now. He's a smart kid and he knows his way around. He'd have found Nana or Citria, or shown up somewhere people know him, like his school."

"We've checked everywhere we can think of that he might go."

Ty heard tears in her voice when she continued. "They must have taken him. Why would anyone take him away?"

Because he saw whoever attacked you, if someone attacked you, and he could identify them. The answer jumped into Ty's mind, but he wasn't about to voice it to Mia. He wasn't sure he was ready to buy into the whole attack story. His heart wanted to believe, but his head and his training told him the tale wasn't likely, given her history.

Mia's voice shrank. "They all believe I did it, don't they? They all think I—I killed my son."

"Mia…" He didn't know what to say. Reassure her, or ask her if they were right? Be her friend—hell more than a friend, or be her doctor? "We'll get to the truth, Mia. We'll figure out what happened to you and to Todd. You just have to hang in there."

"They're going to lock me up again once I'm released from here, aren't they? Nana and Uncle Karl. They're going to make me go back to the loony bin, and this time I'll never get out. I'll never find Todd."

His stomach tumbled. "Maybe it's for the best. You need to rest, you're exhausted and…"

"For the best?" she said harshly, then her voice quieted. "I'll die in there, Ty."

"Mia—"

"Not because I'm going to kill myself, and don't even deny that's what you thought I meant. I will never do that, not while Todd is out there somewhere. Not when he needs me. But because whoever is trying to kill me is eventually going to succeed. I can't protect myself in there."

I'll protect you. The words almost spilled out unbidden. Who was he kidding? Uncle Karl wasn't going to let him near her. Still, he was in too deep to back away. Way too deep. All he had to do was picture her deep, soulful eyes, the thick, dark tumble of wavy hair and he knew he couldn't walk away from her.

"Then fight it," he told her. "You have a right to a competency hearing. Make them plead their case before a judge." He gave her the names of two lawyers, men who'd represented some of Ty's patients in similar proceedings.

Mia promised to call them, and before she hung up eked a promise from Ty to keep looking for Todd. Never to give up.

Damn it, he felt like a Ping-Pong ball. He'd gone from near certainty that Mia wanted to kill herself and take her son to the everlasting with her, to believing she'd been attacked—repeatedly—and her son kidnapped, or worse, in the blink of an eye. Worse, every time he landed on the anti-Mia side, guilt added another lead brick to his gut.

He wanted to believe she was a perfect woman, perfect mother. A mother like he'd never had.

He sighed and rubbed his right temple, soothing the ache building there. The bottom line was, he had to help her. He couldn't stop himself from helping her, even if he wanted to, and his interest wasn't purely professional.

Hell, it wasn't professional at all.

But to help her he needed to get inside her head, and he didn't have the luxury of six months of therapy sessions. He needed to know if she was really a victim here, or if he was making a gargantuan mistake, if he was helping someone who would hurt her own child. Someone like his own mother.

Aw, Christ. Now his head really hurt.

Nana. If anyone knew what was really going on with Mia and Todd, Nana would.

He swung his VW in a U-turn and headed to the Serrat house. Maybe he could kill three birds with one stone. Get a read on Mia's state of mind, convince Nana to ease up on any involuntary commitment plans she was cooking up with Uncle Karl, and pick her brain for more places Todd might go if he was scared. Like if he'd seen his mother unconscious in a running car in a closed garage, and thought she'd killed herself. Wouldn't hurt to dance around the issue of who might want to get rid of Mia, either. Who would benefit from her death. Although he'd have to go easy on that one, since Nana was the most likely candidate to get Mia's money, especially with Todd out of the way, too.

Mulling that thought over in his mind, he pulled up the Serrat drive, shut the car off and started up the walk. The windows were dark and no one answered his repeated raps on the door.

So much for plan A.

Without a plan B to fall back on at the moment, Ty walked back to his car and settled in to wait, still caught up on the thought that if Todd was out of the picture, Mia's beneficiary wouldn't have to worry about trust funds or audits.

Huh.

Shivering, Todd Serrat curled himself into a tighter ball on the musty old comforter; that and his coat were the only things that separated him from the cold concrete floor. His tongue was sticky and his head hurt. He couldn't think straight, but when he heard a sound, he pried his dry eyes open to slits, searching the darkness.

A sliver of light appeared above him, and for a moment he let himself hope. "Mommy?"

But there was no answer, and when the door above him closed, plunging the room back into cold darkness, he squeezed his eyes shut, knowing the heavy footsteps on the stairs weren't Mommy's.

He sniffled and barked at the shadow person. "Go 'way!"

A hand grabbed the shoulder of his jacket and dragged him to a sitting position. He tried to push the shadow person, the black shape in the black room, away, but he was dizzy. "Leave me alone," he whimpered weakly.

Now that he was sitting with his back against a cement-block wall, the shadow person pinched his nose, and when he opened his mouth to breathe, poured a bitter tea down his throat. Todd sputtered and coughed, tried to spit it out, but swallowed enough. Enough, he knew, to make him sleepy again soon.

Tears filled his eyes as he tried to slump down on his side again, but this time the shadow person held him up. His coat was stripped from him, and he pried one eye open. The person in the black hooded sweat-shirt and ski mask pulled out something shiny and grabbed his hand tightly. A second later the knife blade stung his palm and he felt blood run down his fingers.

"Mommy!" he cried, and kicked his feet, tried to

pull his hand away, but the blade cut deeper. He howled, tears flowing freely now. *"Aieee! Mommy!"*

The shadow person was wiping Todd's hand on his coat when the door at the top of the stairs opened, wide this time. Instead of just a flicker as the door opened and closed, a steady shaft of light illuminated a familiar figure in the doorway.

Todd's sleepy eyes flew wide. "Nana?"

Chapter 12

"Ty-baby, come in!" Ty's mother took his hands in hers and pulled him inside, then rubbed her palms over the tops of his hands. "You're freezing! You shouldn't have come out in weather like this, but I'm so glad you're here."

Ty eased his hands out of his mother's grasp. She took his coat by the shoulders, leaving him little choice but to shrug out of it, then hung it in the closet for him. For a moment he wished he could slide back into it and just go, but he really needed to spend some time with his mom. He needed the perspective of a crazy mother who loved her son and yet still hurt him, firsthand.

He'd waited at the Serrat house for almost three

hours, but Nana had never shown up. She was probably out looking for Todd, although he was surprised there was no one at the house in case the boy miraculously found his way home or the police called with news.

By the time he'd finally given up, his stomach was rumbling and he'd run half a tank of gas out of his VW to keep the heater going.

"Come, come sit down," his mom said, waving him out of the foyer of her assisted-living apartment. "Let me make you some tea. Or would you rather have hot chocolate? I think I have some real chocolate, not that packaged stuff."

"No, nothing, Mom."

"Corn chowder, then. I just made a big pot yesterday. I can heat some up."

"I grabbed a burger in the car on the way up."

"Burger, shmurger." She dismissed his protest with a wave. "A growing boy can't survive on fast food. You know how much you love my chowder. It'll only take a minute—"

He stopped her with a hand on her shoulder in the kitchen doorway. "Mom, no." She turned, that crestfallen look on her face that was like a needle in his chest every time it was turned on him.

He recognized the pathology of his behavior. The more his mother doted on him, ingratiated herself to him, the more he rejected her efforts. On the outside he could be the concerned son, even the loving son, but deep down inside, a part of him was still the angry little boy that wanted to punish her for hurting him. But recognizing his behavior and being able to change it were not the same thing.

Gently he turned her toward the living room. "Let's just go sit down, okay? Visit a little."

A soap opera blared on the television. Ty picked up the remote and put it on mute. His mom sat on the end of the floral-print sofa and patted the cushion next to her. He lowered himself into the armchair in front of the window, instead. She sat with her hands in her lap and pulled her lower lip between her teeth.

Sighing at his own belligerence, he slid over next to her. "So how are you, Mom?"

Her eyes lit up. "Oh, fine. You know they take care of everything here. Mrs. Dunbar fell and broke her hip last week, so I've been helping her get along, watering her plants and such. The Kelly brothers in building four moved out—not by their choice, I don't think. They just weren't getting on here. Seems strange. They were always perfect gentlemen around me, but I heard they were harassing the female staff and not taking their medications and such."

Ty listened patiently to the rest of the gossip on his mother's neighbors, then they talked about her "sessions" with her doctor—she refused to call it therapy or treatment. Ty took his time getting around to the conversation he really wanted to have. One he should probably have had with her ten years ago.

"Hey, you know what I did the other day?" he

said. "I went sledding. Haven't done that since I was a kid, you know. You remember how much I used to love sledding?"

"You would have pitched a tent and lived at the top of that hill when it snowed, if I'd have let you."

"Yeah, that was my favorite getaway. And sometimes I really needed to get away." He looked her square in the eyes, gauging her reaction. "You know…from the other stuff."

She didn't take the hook. "I remember one time you stayed out there so long it got dark and I had to come looking for you. I was so worried."

He pressed a little harder. "Yep, and then when we got home you locked me in a closet for fourteen hours because I didn't hang up my coat."

Her smile fell. She stumbled over her words. "Why—I—"

"You said if I had such an aversion to using closets that I could just live in one for a while."

She clutched a fist to her chest. "I never—"

"It was dark in there, and I got really hungry, and had to go to the bathroom. But you remember what happened when I tried to come out? Do you remember what you did to me? How you hurt me?"

"Ty! Stop it! Why on earth would you say something like that? Ty-baby, I love you. I would never be so cruel to you. I would never hurt you!"

She said it with such conviction, and with such pain on her face that if he hadn't known better, he might have believed her. He knew she loved him.

He also knew what she'd done to him, even if she didn't. He didn't think she was lying—not in the traditional sense. She really believed what she was saying.

He had his answer. Could a mother hurt, maybe even kill, her own child and be so deluded that she could not only convince others, but herself that she hadn't done it?

Yes.

He'd always known this, but he'd had to check. Had to be sure. Because if it was true, if his mother could look and sound so honest when she denied what she'd done—if she could actually believe she hadn't done it—then so could Mia Serrat.

He lowered his head and scrubbed his palms across his face. "Yeah, Mom. Sorry."

When he looked up, struggling to return to any kind of normal conversation, he noticed that the news had broken into the soap opera. The headline Breaking News scrolled across the top of the screen and Todd Serrat's picture was in a little window in the corner. It looked like the reporter who had raked Mia's name through the mud earlier was doing another live report from the hospital.

Ty grabbed the remote control and put the sound back on.

"…Marika Towne reporting live for News Nine here at the Eternal Emergency Care Clinic where the mother of the missing eight-year-old boy, Todd Serrat, is about to be discharged."

The anchor at the studio news desk chimed in.

"The mother is the prime suspect in her son's disappearance, right?"

"That's right, Chet, according to our sources in the sheriff's department, she's the only suspect at this time, and a three-way battle between the Serrat family, Ms. Serrat and her lawyer, and the police is being waged here over her immediate future. The family has asked a judge to commit her to a mental health facility, but Ms. Serrat and her lawyer are contesting that request. Meanwhile, the police would like to have her come stay in their facility—the county jail—but say they don't have enough evidence yet to file charges, though they are considering detaining her pursuant to the investigation. Despite the protests of her family and the police's suspicions, it appears this possible child-murdering mom is about to walk off scot-free."

Ty clicked the power off and the TV screen went blank. "I've got to go, Mom."

Mia pulled her shoulders back and her chin up before she stepped out the glass doors of the emergency clinic and into the frigid Massachusetts sunshine where a bevy of cameras and microphones awaited. Several more crews had joined the News Nine group she'd glimpsed earlier.

A dozen questions were shouted before the door had closed behind her. She'd almost made it through the crowd without reacting when the last question stopped her.

"Mia, did you kill your son?"

Her blood ran as cold as the snow that lay like a freshly laundered blanket on the ground. "My son is the love of my life. I would never hurt him. Ever."

She knew she shouldn't have responded to the reporters, shouldn't have stopped. Getting one answer only increased the fervor of the feeding frenzy. The camera crews closed in around her to get close-ups, blocking her way. The reporters shouted more questions, more accusations.

She shouldered her way through, shaking her head to say she wouldn't speak again, and bit her lip to hold her resolve—and her stoic expression—in place. She was never so glad to see anything as she was to see Ty's beat-up VW pulling up to the curb as she made her way past the last newsman. She walked around and got in the passenger side without question and he pulled back onto the roadway. Only then did she let herself slump.

Her chest rattled as she took a deep breath.

Ty cut his gaze off the road a second to check her out. "You okay?"

She nodded, swallowing hard. She was fine except that her little boy was missing, no one believed someone was trying to kill her and she was about to be committed, arrested or both. "The wolves are circling, but thanks to the lawyer you recommended, they're not biting. Yet."

Ty flexed his fingers on the steering wheel. "Mia, who gets your money if you're out of the picture?"

The question took her by surprise. She paused, then understood. "No, you can't mean this is happening because someone is after my money."

"Why not?"

"Because it would all go to Todd."

"And if he were out of the picture?"

"Oh, God." She bit her lip. "No. No. Nana is my beneficiary. She would never hurt Todd. No. He's just scared. He's run away. Hiding."

Ty drove in silence a few moments. She couldn't tell if he believed her or not. "So what now?"

"I have to find Todd. I need to go home and get my car and look for him."

"Where are you going to look?"

"Anywhere. *Everywhere.* I don't know."

"You can't just drive around aimlessly hoping to catch a glimpse of him."

She could do exactly that, if there was nothing else to be done. Desperation could make her do a lot of crazy things. "I can't just sit around doing nothing."

"You can go home, rest, eat."

"No, I don't think I can," she said quietly.

Ty frowned at her, then turned his gaze back to the road. "The police are doing everything that can be done. There's nothing—"

"That's not what I mean." She paused a heartbeat, quelling the panic that threatened to rise. "Nana signed the commitment request with Karl, didn't she. She's trying to have me put away."

She knew she was right when Ty didn't deny it.

She lowered her head. "Then I don't have a home to go to."

He took one hand off the steering wheel, reached across the seat and laid his palm over her fingers. "Yes, you do," he said gruffly, then cut another look over at her. "You can come home with me."

Chapter 13

Mia hesitated on the threshold to Ty's apartment. "Maybe this isn't a good idea."

"Mia, we've been driving around for hours. We've checked and rechecked all the places you thought Todd might go. Eventually you have to stop. Sleep. Let the police do their jobs."

He prodded her forward from behind, but she held her ground. Her gaze took in the battered brown leather couch, the coffee table littered with thick books—textbooks, they looked like—yellow pads of paper and pens, the running shoes lying sideways in the middle of the floor as though they'd just been kicked off, the dirty plate and fork next to another stack of textbooks on the two-seater dining table against the wall, the sweatshirt thrown over the back of a chair. Some might call it messy, but to her it was…unpretentious. Homey. Cozy, even.

And small. The two of them would be sharing very close quarters, and she wasn't sure either one of them was ready for that.

"That's not what I meant," she said. Looking up at him, she saw he understood. But it was too late. They were beyond the point of no return.

"Come on." He went around her shoulder and pulled her inside, then hurried through the room scooping up dishes, clothes and an empty soda can as he went.

She studied the books on the dining table. *Modern Mental Models. Pathology of Traumatic Brain Injury and Corresponding Emotional Disorders. The Physician's Desk Reference.* Just a little light reading for his evenings, she guessed, and traced a finger over the well-worn spine of the desk reference. "Uncle Karl is not going to like this."

"Don't worry about him."

"You could be risking your career."

He dropped the dishes in the sink, the can in the trash and tossed the clothes behind a folding door she assumed hid the laundry facilities, then he turned to her and shrugged. "Actually, I think my career is already pretty much trashed."

"I'm sorry." Was she destined to destroy every life she touched?

"Hey, not because of you. That's not what I

meant." He shrugged. "Karl's pretty much had it in for me since day one."

"So I'll just be the final nail in the coffin. I feel much better about that, then." Sarcasm dripped through the words, and he rolled his eyes.

"How about something to eat? I've got…" He opened the refrigerator door, then closed it and moved to a cabinet. "Oatmeal?"

"You eat oatmeal for supper?"

"I do when there's nothing else in the house. I have maple syrup to go on it, though."

"Oatmeal it is, then." Though she wasn't the least bit hungry, she needed at least to pretend some level of normalcy.

Five minutes later, he had cleared the books from the dining table and they sat across from each other with steaming bowls of lumpy cereal in front of them. The silence was deafening.

"Kind of awkward, huh?"

He peered at her over a heaping spoonful of oatmeal dripping with syrup. "Doesn't seem right just to make small talk with everything that's going on."

"And all the serious topics we should be discussing are too depressing for my fragile state."

"I didn't say that."

"You didn't have to."

He set his spoon down. "You want to talk about Todd, fine. Let's talk."

She shook her head. Her chest had grown almost too tight to speak at the mere mention of her son's name. "No, you're right. There's nothing to say that hasn't been said already." She managed a small, fake smile. "Thanks for trying, though. And for putting up with me. I know I'm kind of a wreck right now. It's just that it's getting dark outside, and I'm sitting here nice and warm and comfortable with a man who—" She pressed her lips into a firm line. "With a friend. And I keep thinking that maybe Todd is out there in the cold somewhere, hungry and thinking I've abandoned him. Again."

He was quiet a moment, looked thoughtful, then he reached across the tiny table and took her hand in his. His grip was strong and warm. His fingertips and palms were slightly callused, but the sensation against her own skin was pleasant. Tingly.

"That's just fear talking. Don't let it get the best of you. And don't let it control you." With his other hand he pushed her bowl closer. "Starving yourself won't help, either."

She knew that, but still the sight of food had made her stomach turn. And the warmth of his brown eyes and the way he was slowly rubbing his thumb back and forth across her knuckles was making her stomach flip for an entirely other reason.

After Sam died, she'd thought she'd never feel anything for another man. Had never wanted to, even. Because she never wanted to open herself to the pain of losing another man. Yet even though now was the worst possible time, she was beginning to open herself to possibilities again. But Ty Hansen was her doctor and worked for the man who was trying to commit her. And for that reason, she just couldn't open herself to this possibility.

Regretfully, she eased her hand from beneath Ty's. "I think I'll just lie down a little while. Maybe a nap will settle my stomach."

She stood and he rose alongside her, wiping his hands on the thighs of his jeans. "Sure, you can take the bedroom."

"No, it's too early to call it a night. I want to check in with the sheriff's office later, see if they've got any new leads on Todd. Besides, you'd be hanging over both ends of that couch. I'll sleep out here tonight."

If he had any chivalrous ideas of coercing her to take the bed, he kept them to himself. But he did bring her a pillow and a soft, fleecy blanket. When he tucked the cover under her chin and told her "Sweet dreams," her heart swelled with longing to touch the curve of his lips with her fingertips, to trace the stubbled line of his chin.

Instead she closed her eyes and curled her fingers in the blanket, but the memory of his face, so close to hers, his breath, maple-syrup sweet, fanning her cheeks, stayed in her mind long into sleep.

When she woke, the lights were dimmed, but she could see that the dishes were done and put away, the books and papers had been stacked neatly in a corner, and soft music rolled from a CD player on the table by the door. It was an acoustic guitar piece, instrumental only, slow and soothing.

She wiped the sleep from her eyes and got up, absently picked up the CD case to see who the artist was, and heard Ty's murmuring voice coming from the bedroom. He sat facing away from her on the navy-blue comforter that covered his bed, his shirt and shoes off, his cell phone to his ear.

"That's bull, Chuck," he said. Chuck? That was his friend in the sheriff's office's name, if she remembered right. She leaned against the doorjamb, afraid to breathe. Had they gotten some news on Todd?

Ty shook his head as if his friend on the phone could see him. "If the D.A. had a case, circumstantial or otherwise, he'd file charges."

There was a pause while Ty listened.

"Yeah, what was all that crap on TV about 'sources in the sheriff's office,' anyway?" Pause. "Has it occurred to you that they're leaking the information just to incriminate Mia in the press? They're making noise to cover their asses because they have no idea what happened to her son."

Longer pause. Ty pinched the bridge of his nose. "I didn't say that." He listened. "I didn't say I *don't* believe her, either."

Mia inhaled sharply. Ty heard her and twisted around to see her. His face darkened. "Just keep me informed if you hear anything. I gotta go."

He flipped the phone shut. "Mia."

"It's all right." She preempted whatever he was going to say. Whatever explanation he might make. "It's not like I didn't realize you still don't believe me."

"I'm not sure what to believe, Mia. I've never lied to you about that."

She cocked her head to one side, the ache in her chest easing a bit. "What surprises me is that you're still helping me, even though you aren't sure."

He got up and walked to stand directly in front of her. He stared at her, and the intensity of his scrutiny made her realize she must look a mess with her hair all tousled from sleep and her clothes wrinkled. Self-consciously she raised a hand to straighten the collar of her blouse and he took it, lowered it.

"Yeah," he said, his voice husky as he pushed past her into the other room. "Surprises me, too, sometimes."

Ty paced the length of his living room—about four steps—and back again.

Damn, he had to get over this thing with Mia, and he had to do it fast. Like before she ran out of hot water and stepped out of his shower.

Maybe she had been right about this being a bad idea, though the biggest problem had nothing to do with Karl, and everything to do with the fact that sharing a tiny apartment was too…intimate. He was too close to her, too aware of all the little details of life, like how amazing she looked, all soft and rumpled from sleep, her hair falling over her eyes and her shirt pulled far enough over one shoulder that he could see the elegant curve of her collarbone.

Yes, this was definitely a bad idea, but what could he do about it? He could take her to a hotel, but that would be worse. He couldn't leave her alone, not right now. She didn't have anyone else.

Neither did he, a little voice in his head said. Not anyone like Mia. Maybe he never would.

The way she'd reacted to overhearing him say he didn't believe her had surprised him. She hadn't broken down, hadn't cried, hadn't protested her innocence. She'd simply accepted. She'd even had enough perspective on the situation to see it from a point of view other than her own and realize the contradiction in his behavior. Definitely not typical mental-patient behavior. More like a sure sign that she was stronger than everyone thought. Maybe even stronger than *she* thought.

And that was what tied him in knots.

The drumming of the shower quit, and with it, Ty's time ran out. No doubt in another life he'd do whatever it took to make Mia a permanent fixture in his life and his bed.

Unfortunately, he was stuck in this life. And Mia Serrat was unreachable. Untouchable, at least by him.

Fortifying himself with a deep breath, he picked up the T-shirt and sweatpants he'd pulled out of his dresser a few minutes ago and went to the bathroom door, ready to hand them to her and then lock himself in his room for the night. Alone.

What he wasn't ready for was the sight of her wearing nothing but a towel, her hair piled on top of her head in some sort of self-knotting twist, her bare shoulders moist and glowing from the heat of the shower.

His throat went dry and his legs turned to cast iron. He couldn't move them.

She almost ran into him before she saw him in the doorway. They stood toe to toe, so close he could feel the heat rising from her skin. So close he could see the same heat in her eyes. Eyes that were locked on him.

She found the strength to pull her gaze away first, and with the broken—or at least loosened—connection between them, he found his voice. "I, uh, brought you something to wear. They're clean." He lifted the shirt to his nose and sniffed. "I think."

She smiled and took the bundle from his arms, but neither of them moved.

"I want to believe you," he finally said, breaking a long silence, and had no idea where the words had come from, even though he recognized them as the truth. He hadn't consciously decided to admit that to her.

"Shh," she said, and put a finger to his lips. "Don't."

Her finger was rose-petal soft on his mouth, and he wanted to pull it inside, devour it, taste it. Taste her. Instead he shifted just a little, just enough to brush the pad a little harder. A whisper of a kiss.

She swayed with the sensation, bringing her closer, and lowered her hand slowly. They were almost touching. If she raised up just a little, or if he lowered his head, he could have a real kiss. The need was so strong that it coiled inside him, twisted like a fist around his gut.

He wasn't sure who moved, who gave in to the temptation first, but a moment later they were pressed hip to hip, chest to chest, lips to lips. She was as sweet as he'd dreamed she would be. Not candy-store sugary sweet, but heady, like a deep red wine, and just as potent. His head started to spin and he couldn't get enough of her. He wrapped himself around her, legs, arms, and took the kiss deeper.

She framed his face with her hands and took back as much as she gave. She made a sound low in her throat and he felt the knot on the towel give way between them. Only the crush of their bodies held it in place, and he took advantage of the droop of the terry behind her back to skim his hands across her shoulder blades, up and down her spine. Her skin was as smooth as a baby's, and every spot he touched trembled beneath his fingertips.

Her hands moved from his face to his waist, skimmed around the top of his jeans, and his own muscles fluttered in response. It was as if her hands were electricity and he was a live wire. Her touch flowed through him as much as over him.

He moaned, liking the sensation. Liking it way too much. Finally he had to come up for air, and with the return of oxygen to his brain came the return of reason.

He buried his face against the crook of her neck,

felt her pulse spurt beneath his lips and nearly lost his resolve. Again.

"Aw, Mia." He held her close, not ready to let her go, yet knowing he would have to. Soon. "We can't."

Chapter 14

Mia plummeted from the heights of passion to the depths of despair in less than the span of a heartbeat. It felt so good in his arms. So warm, so comfortable, so…right.

And so wrong.

The cool air that brushed her damp skin with its chill fingers as he pulled himself away felt cold. Lonely.

Her towel slipped and she caught it embarrassingly low with one arm across her chest. The ends flapped open behind her.

"You're right. Of course," she mumbled, wiping her damp hair back from her face. "I don't know what I was thinking."

He shoved his fingers in the pockets of his jeans.

"I don't think either of us were thinking. That's the point."

"How could I have…almost…with Todd missing? God, what kind of mother am I?"

He caught her by her shoulders as she tried to brush past. To get away from him, from the accusation she was afraid she'd see in his eyes. "That's not what I meant."

She turned, silently questioning.

"We're both worried about Todd. But there is nothing either one of us can do for him right now. All we can do is wait and have faith. At least until we have something more to go on."

"There has to be something I can do."

His grip on her shoulders tightened. His hands were warm and her bare skin tingled beneath his touch.

"There's not," he said.

She looked up at him through her lashes, trying to gauge his sincerity. "Then why did you…stop?"

"I'm sorry." He drew a deep breath. "I just can't."

The fact that she'd just been rejected finally penetrated her sluggish mind. "*Can't,* can't? Or *won't,* can't?"

"Can't is can't."

"And won't is won't. There is a big difference between the two."

"Mia, you're my patient."

"Not any longer."

"That's debatable." He dragged his hand through his hair, making it stick up in all directions. He jolted a little, as if he'd gotten a static shock, and his gaze lingered over her shoulder.

Belatedly she realized he was probably getting a fine view of her ass in the vanity mirror and reached her free hand around to try to pull the ends of the towel together. After a moment of flailing behind her, she thought the hell with it and let the towel go altogether.

She didn't get the reaction she'd hoped for. He was more prepared this time. Slowly he bent over and picked up the clothes she'd dropped somewhere in the middle of his kiss and held them out to her.

His gaze fixed firmly on her face, he said. "It's not me you want, Mia. It's a warm body to hold. Safety. Security."

Now that made her mad. "Stop analyzing me, *Doc.*"

He didn't respond, so she snatched the clothes from him and tugged them on just for something to do. Anything but look at him. Anything but think about him.

He turned and walked away, and she followed him, still stewing, and stumbled over the left leg of the sweatpants that she was still trying to pull on. He stopped at the refrigerator, pulled out a beer and snapped off the top, then sat on the couch.

She followed and sat in the chair by the window, composing her thoughts. "Have you ever been married, Ty?"

"No." He took a swig of beer.

She nodded seriously. "I guess you're a virgin, then. That's the problem."

He choked. "Hardly."

"You've been desperately in love with every woman you slept with?"

The way she had been, was, with Sam.

She pushed that thought aside. She would love Sam forever, but this wasn't about him. It hadn't been about Sam for a long time.

She had his interest; she could see that in his eyes, the way he spun the bottle in the palm of one hand.

"Did you want to marry every one of your lovers? Raise babies with them and grow gray hair with them?"

Of course he hadn't.

"Make your point," he said.

"The point is," she said carefully. "Sometimes a warm body is enough. And if you get a little safety and security in the deal, so much the better."

He narrowed his eyes.

"If you don't want me, all I ask is that you say so. Don't hide behind excuses, lie about it because you think I can't take the truth."

He set his beer on the coffee table and leaned forward, resting his elbows on his knees. "Honey, if I told you I didn't want you...*that* would be the lie."

Warmth pooled in her chest like hot wax around the wick of a burning candle. He rose and held his hand out to her. She rose and took it. "Where are we going?"

"To the one place we've both wanted to be since the moment we met." Flames kindled in the dark depths of his eyes. "To bed."

* * *

Ty stood face-to-face with Mia beside his bed and stripped the T-shirt he'd given her only a few minutes ago over her head. He lifted one perfect, rose-tipped breast in his palm and studied it like a man who had never seen a woman before.

He'd never seen a woman like Mia before, as beautiful inside as she was out.

He dipped his head and tongued her nipple, savoring his first taste. "You're going to hate me in the morning."

"No."

"Next week, then, or next year."

"Never."

He moved his head to her right side and swirled his tongue around the flat nipple, raising it to a tight peak. "Fine. I'll just hate myself, then."

She laughed. "That I could give you some pointers on." Her hands channeled through his hair, holding his head close. Not that he needed holding. He wasn't going anywhere.

Her head tipped back and all that gorgeous, thick hair of hers flowed down her back, over his hands. He wrapped it around his fist and raised his head to capture her mouth. She was as sweet as he remembered. Sweet and intoxicating.

Her palms roamed restlessly over his back, down to the waistband of his jeans and up to his shoulders. Her nails skimmed his sensitized skin, feeding the fire inside him.

With one hand behind her head and the other on the small of her back he cradled her as he pushed her back to the mattress, softened her impact and then caught himself before his weight crushed her.

"I probably should have mentioned this while I still had all my clothes on," she said, and bit her lip before continuing. "I'm a really bad bet, you know. My life is a wreck. I'm living on borrowed time before I end up in the slammer or the nuthouse— odds are even which one."

Her arguments weren't distracting him from his mission, which was to slide the unflattering U of MA sweatpants off her long, long legs. One thing about him...once he set a course, a hurricane couldn't steer him away. "Then we shouldn't waste any time."

Mission accomplished. She hooked one bare leg over his hip and rubbed the back of his thigh with her foot.

He reached back, grabbed her ankle and pulled it over his shoulder. She got the idea and her other leg looped over his other shoulder. He scooted down the mattress and lowered his forehead to rest on her navel, drawing out the moment.

Once he crossed this line, there was no going back.

She reached down and stroked his cheek with the back of her hand. When he looked up, he realized— the hell with it—he didn't want to go back. Ever.

He pulled her folds apart and touched her with his tongue, sucked her with his lips, dove deep into her recesses. She writhed beneath him, moaned and fisted the bedsheets. Her hips jerked up and he rode her mounting frenzy relentlessly, pushing her farther, harder, than he'd ever pushed any woman before, because he knew she could take it. Instinctively he knew she would take everything he had to give, and return it in spades.

He used his fingers to drive deeper and her breathing went fast and shallow, her bucking grew wilder. Her head thrashed from side to side on the pillow, throwing her dark hair across her ivory-skinned face.

"Ty. Please," she begged. She pleaded. She demanded.

And he delivered. He rose above her, braced on his forearms and plunged deep. Her full mouth rounded into a shocked O. Her eyes stared sightlessly and her breath shuddered.

His own body mirrored her shock, stunning him thoughtless, mindless with the pleasure. Their bodies fitted as if they'd been made for each other. As if they'd once been a single being, separated at birth and now celebrating at being reunited.

It felt right. *She* felt right. He'd never experienced a more perfect moment, a moment in which he knew he'd been wrong when he'd accused her earlier of wanting safety and security.

He was the one who wanted those things. Needed them. And he'd found them in her. That and much more.

As soon as he'd been old enough to cross the street by himself, he'd tried to stay away from his mother as much as possible. He'd lived as a nomad, spending long hours at the houses of friends, in the library, on the street corner. He'd never considered the place where he lived anything other than a house or an apartment. A place to keep his stuff and to avoid as much as possible.

Now, at twenty-six years of age, he'd finally found home, and it had nothing to do with where he lived and everything to do with who he was with.

He began to move and Mia fell in perfect rhythm with him. They breathed in tempo. Muscles tensed and relaxed in synch. Hot, damp skin slid across hot, damp skin. The only sound in the room was the slap of their bodies, the creak of the bed and their harsh breaths, and the sound of their lovemaking was as moving as a Mozart concerto.

He thrust faster, deeper, his pulse pounding like a bass drum, feeling himself spinning out of control. Her back arched off the bed, lifting him. Her fingers dug deep into his shoulders and she cried his name.

The wet heat of her body grabbed him, pulled him over the edge of sanity with her, and then he was the one crying out, a roar of pure male satisfaction. Of possession.

When his arms wouldn't hold his weight a second longer, he collapsed to her side. Gradually their heavy breathing returned to normal.

When he threw an arm behind his head, he noticed the window over the bed. The curtains were open, but he didn't think anyone on the street could have seen what had just happened between him and Mia. The heat of their bodies had fogged the glass.

She turned to her side and pillowed her head on his shoulder. Words weren't necessary. Their bodies had said everything.

He fell asleep to the soft sough of her breath in his ears, the scent of her hair in his nostrils, and the feel of her drawing light circles through the hair on his chest.

His awakening was much less gentle. Someone was pounding on the front door and shouting. Still half asleep, he was on his feet and had his jeans pulled on before it dawned on him what the voices were saying.

"Sheriff's department! Open up!"

Mia sat up in bed, clutching the sheet to her chest with one hand. With the other she pushed a wave of dark hair off her face. Her eyes were glassy with fear.

"Stay here," he told her and started for the door. The deputies shouted again, and he answered, "Just a second, I'm coming."

Four cops stood in the hall when he opened the door. His stomach fell. Four. That couldn't be good. The one in front slid the police baton he'd been using to rap on the door back into a loop on his belt. "Dr. Ty Hansen?" he asked.

"Yes."

"Is Ms. Mia Serrat here on these premises?"

"Why—" he started, but never got to finish the question. Mia appeared in the hallway behind him, wearing the T-shirt he'd given her earlier. The thin white cotton draped to mid-thigh on her, but did little to disguise the enticing shape beneath.

The cops pushed past him. He stopped the last one with a hand on the man's shoulder as he passed. "What the hell is going on?"

The man he stopped didn't answer. The burly cop in front, the one who'd had the baton, told him all he needed to know when he pulled out a pair of silver handcuffs. "Ms. Serrat, I have a warrant for your arrest."

Ty started toward her.

Her shoulders shook visibly, but her voice was steady. "What's the charge?"

"Murder."

"Oh my God. Todd? You found Todd. Is he—?" Her face went as white as the T-shirt she had on, and Ty reached her side just in time to catch her as she fell.

Chapter 15

"How can they charge her with murder if they don't have a body?" Ty propped his elbows on Chuck Campbell's desk and buried his face in his hands, trying to rub away the sleepiness. It had been a long night in the Eternal sheriff's office lobby, waiting for some word on what was happening with Mia. Now the sun was rising outside the eastern window, and he still wasn't sure.

"It's uncommon, but there is precedent. Nine-year-olds don't just leave bloody jackets behind and go missing by themselves."

"Eight."

"What?"

He sighed, straightened up. "Todd Serrat is eight years old."

Chuck tapped the eraser end of a pencil on his desk. "*Was* eight years old, it looks like."

"So they found Todd's jacket with blood on it. It doesn't prove anything."

"It proves she was lying about him being in the house while she was supposedly attacked in the garage. I told you, the jacket was found in the woods near the sledding hill by some kids playing. Todd Serrat never made it home that day."

"It's circumstantial, at best."

"A lot of criminals get put away on circumstantial evidence. Can you just admit for once that this case really is as simple—and as sad—as it seems on the surface? That she's been playing you all along, and that there's something wrong in her head that makes her want to hurt herself and her son?"

Ty's stomach burned from too much coffee and not enough sleep. He didn't want to admit it, even to himself, much less to Chuck, because if it was true, if Mia had done this, then the best night of his life was also the biggest mistake of his life.

He rubbed the back of his neck, sighed. "It's possible."

Chuck's chair creaked as the deputy leaned back and propped a booted foot on his desk. "Would have done yourself a lot of good if you'd come to that realization before you slept with her, buddy."

"Back off, *buddy.*"

Chuck held up his hands. "All right, none of my business. I'm just sayin'…"

"Can you get me in to see her?"

Chuck's booted foot clomped to the floor. His chair creaked again. "Actually, I was hoping you'd ask that."

Ty lowered his hand warily. "Why?"

"Because she trusts you. You're the only one who has a chance of getting through to her. The detectives got squat when they interviewed her. The State Bureau of Investigation couldn't even get her to look at them." He leveled a hard gaze at Ty. "We need a confession, man."

"Screw you." He lurched to his feet, knocking his chair over in the process.

"No, screw that kid. Because that's what you'll be doing if you walk away from this."

Blood drummed in Ty's ears.

Chuck walked around the desk and stood next to him. "I know this case hits close to home for you," he said quietly. "And I'm sorry no one was there to stand up for you when you needed it, including me. I knew what was going on. I could have told a teacher, a cop. Someone."

Ty cut his gaze away. They'd never talked about what had happened to him all those years ago. Some things just didn't need to be said between friends. "You were just a kid yourself. And I made you swear."

"Yeah, to an oath I have regretted keeping every day."

Ty shrugged, his shoulders stiff. "Old news, Chuck. What does any of this have to do with Mia?"

"If there is even the slightest chance that kid is still alive, then he's hurt and she's got him stashed somewhere. We need to know where. We've got to find him before it's too late." Chuck put his hand on Ty's shoulder. "I'm sorry there was no one there to pull you out of the hell you were living in. But we have a chance to pull Todd Serrat out of his hell if he's still alive. Are you gonna walk away from that?"

Ty's eyes burned with exhaustion and emotion. He tilted his head back and stared at the ceiling. "No."

"I didn't think so." Chuck clapped him on the back and nodded down the hall. "We'd better get a move on. We're only going to get one shot at this."

Ty followed Chuck toward the lockup. "Why?"

"Because she's still in an interrogation room for now, so we can keep an eye on her through the two-way mirror. She's being transferred in a few hours."

"Transferred where?"

Chuck stopped to key open the door to a corridor lined with jail cells on either side ending in an unmarked door. "The mental health hospital. Family got the judge to reconsider the commitment petition based on the new evidence."

Ty snorted. "I should've seen that one coming."

Mia sat in the interrogation room fingering a scratch in the heavy varnish of the conference table in the middle of the room. Her back ached from hours of sitting here with the rungs of the chair digging into her spine, but she didn't move, didn't shift. She wouldn't give whoever was watching her from the other side of the two-way mirror the satisfaction of seeing her discomfort.

Bastards. They thought she'd killed her son. How could anyone think that? How could anyone accuse her of that? Every minute they wasted questioning her was a minute they weren't out there looking for Todd. Bile rose in her throat to think about her baby out there alone, scared, hurt, or God forbid, worse. Outwardly she sat still, quiet, but inside her stomach twisted and burned.

The door opened behind her, and she angled her head just enough to see Ty slip into the room. He looked rumpled and tired and she'd never seen a more welcome sight in her life.

"Oh, thank God." She stood up, raised her arms to him, but he stiffened and drew back.

Her arms fell uselessly to her sides. "Ty?"

He moved to the end of the conference table, sat and picked at the scratches much as she had been doing.

The wind gushed out of her and she slumped back into her chair. He laced his fingers restlessly and looked up at her. "We don't have much time, Mia."

"I know," she said quietly. When he didn't continue, she filled the silence. "You think I did it, don't you? You said you weren't decided before. Now you are. You think I hurt my own son."

His jaw was harder than she remembered, even

shadowed with soft blond stubble. The creases fanning out from his eyes were deeper. "I think you love your son. I don't think you *want* to hurt him."

She slapped her palms flat on the table. Hot tears burned behind her eyes. "The poor crazy lady just can't help herself though, huh? Is that it? First I try to kill myself and now my son?"

"Look, I really do believe that you love Todd, on some level."

"Some level?" A sick laugh gurgled in her throat.

He forged on. "And I really wish we had all the time in the world to sort out what you're feeling—"

"Oh, please."

"—to help you. But we don't have time for that."

"Then why are you here?"

"To help Todd."

Her eyes felt too large for her face as she stared at him. "How?"

He took a deep breath and let it out slowly, once again the professional in control. "Tell me what happened after I left the park."

She hissed, physically pained to have to explain it again. To him. "Todd and I got in the car and I drove home. I pulled into the garage, and Todd went into the house." She drilled a hole in him with her gaze. "He was *wearing* his coat. Then someone grabbed me from behind and tried to kill me—"

"How did the coat get back to the park?" he interrupted.

"I don't know. Maybe whoever took him planted it there to put suspicion on me."

"It's all part of the grand conspiracy, huh? First someone is trying to kill you, and now they're trying to frame you. Which is it?"

"I don't know." Her head felt too heavy for her neck. Sometimes her story sounded crazy, even to her. "Oh, God. Maybe some pedophile followed us home and snatched him."

"I need you to think, Mia. Think about what really happened."

"That *is* what really happened."

"They're going to take you back to the hospital in a little while, Mia. You know what it will be like there. They'll put you on meds. This might be your last chance for a long time to talk to someone while your head is clear. If you really love Todd, you will tell me the truth."

"I *am* telling you the truth."

"Tell me where he is."

"I don't know where he is!"

He leaned forward, kept pressing her, rapid-fire. "Look, Mia. Whatever happened, whatever you did—"

She lurched to her feet, feeling sick, dizzy. "Son of a bitch." She was shouting now, didn't care. "You don't know. You have no idea what it's like to be a mother."

She spun away, faced the wall. Didn't hear him come up behind her through the clamor of her thundering pulse.

"No," he said grimly, turning her around by her

arm. "But I know something about mothers who love their sons, and yet still manage to hurt them. Look."

He pushed his right sleeve up his arm. She tried to turn away, but he held her wrist in a grip like a vise.

"Look," he commanded.

She remembered the scars. The crisscrossed white lines, the circles. He'd said he'd been caught in a piece of machinery as a kid.

"I don't understand."

"My mother loved me. I really believe she did. Does."

Understanding dawned horribly as Mia watched the memories scroll across his face.

"That didn't stop her from slicing me with a razor blade whenever the mood struck her. Or burning me with cigarettes or just knocking me upside the head."

"Oh my God." The pain he must have suffered, the torture—it was unimaginable that anyone could put a little boy through that. But that didn't mean that she would do the same.

She eased her arm out of his grip. "I am not your mother."

"No," he said, meeting her gaze squarely as he let her go. "At least I survived my mother's abuse."

Crack!

Her palm connected with his cheek before she realized she was moving.

He hardly flinched, just drilled her with his honeyed eyes. "I believe you just made my point."

Her fists clenched at her sides. The tears that had

burned behind her eyes swelled around her eyelids. "Screw you."

"You already did that."

She blanched. Making love with Ty had been the only thing that felt right, that felt *real* about this whole week. Now that memory had turned into something ugly, too.

A knock on the door broke the strained silence between them. The deputy poked his head in and looked at Ty. "Time."

Ty turned a sad face on her. "Last chance. Please let me help Todd, and you. Tell me where he is."

She shook her head. Her voice broke. "I don't know."

As Ty shuffled out of the room with the deputy, her tears finally spilled over.

She would never hurt her son. Couldn't. Far-fetched as it sounded, someone had tried to kill her and had taken him. That was what had really happened, whether anyone believed her or not.

Chapter 16

Ty stepped out of the interrogation room just as the next door in the hall—the door to the room on the other side of Mia's two-way mirror—opened. Karl Serrat stepped out, flanked on either side by attendants from the hospital. His face was an angry red and his lips were set in a narrow line. He stood chest to chest with Ty. "I hope you said your goodbyes."

"I said what I needed to say to Mia." Ty could hear Chuck shuffling his feet on the floor behind him.

"I meant at the hospital. You won't be going back. You, Dr. Hansen, are fired. With extreme prejudice. Fired."

Karl shouldered past and into the interrogation

room while Ty stood rooted in place. He must have heard everything, he realized. Everything.

"Let's go." Chuck nudged him from behind. "You don't need to see this."

This. The Kaiser and his goons taking Mia away. Would they put her in handcuffs? Strap her to a gurney?

Ty made a beeline for the men's room and heaved into the urinal. When his legs were almost steady again, Chuck was waiting outside the door with a cold soda. Ty followed him to the deputy's desk and sat heavily.

Chuck leaned back in his chair and put his feet up. "You pressed her pretty hard, buddy."

"You're the one who made it clear a kid's life is at stake."

"Yeah." Chuck lowered his gaze. "Still…"

Ty sighed. "Yeah."

Not all of his bad attitude in the interrogation room had been about Mia or Todd, though he hated to admit it. He'd let it get personal. About him. The anger of his childhood he'd thought he'd buried long ago had seeped to the surface and mingled with the hurt feelings of his present. The sense that Mia had betrayed him somehow by making him care about her and then doing something so heinous as hurting her own son.

"Well, since it looks like your career as a psychiatrist is in the crapper, maybe I can get you on here. You're one hell of an interrogator."

Ty rolled his eyes over the rim of his pop can. "Not funny."

Chuck cocked his head. "You okay?"

"Not even close."

The deputy dropped his feet back to the floor. "If your stomach is rightside up now, how about we go out and get something stronger than soda? I'm buying."

The last thing Ty wanted was to be around a lot of noise and people. He shook his head. "I gotta go."

"Yeah, that empty apartment of yours really needs you. Better hurry."

Ty smiled a little at that. "I appreciate the offer, Chuck, but I need some time."

At least a few centuries, he thought as he walked out of the sheriff's office.

Maybe longer.

After Ty left, Chuck Campbell started in on his paperwork. Reports for this, reports for that. Reports explaining why his other reports were late. Damned if some days he didn't feel more like a secretary than a cop. He hadn't even made a dent in the stack of forms in his inbox when a shadow loomed over his desk.

"Deputy." The gloomy figure looming over him greeted him sourly.

"Mr. Serrat. I thought you'd left. Is there a problem with your niece's transfer?" *Probably someone didn't do the right paperwork,* he thought sardonically.

"No. She's been sedated and the orderlies will accompany her to the hospital. I need to speak to you about another matter, if I may."

Chuck set down his pen. "Sure."

Ten minutes later, he pulled a pack of spearmint gum from his breast pocket, unwrapped a piece and popped it in his mouth. "Curiouser and curiouser."

"What is that supposed to mean?" Karl Serrat stiffened on the other side of Chuck's desk. The deputy offered the man a piece of gum, but Karl declined.

Chuck tapped the missing person's report the doc had just finished filling out on his sister, Nana. "Doesn't it seem strange to you that two people from the same family have gone mysteriously missing in less than a week, and a third is reporting multiple murder attempts on her person?"

Chuck hadn't thought it possible, but Karl's back straightened even further. "You think that Nana's disappearance and Todd's are related?"

"Seems likely."

Karl's perpetually stern expression became even more menacing. "Mia's whereabouts are pretty well accounted for since Nana was last seen. She was either here or with Dr. Hansen the whole time."

"You're assuming Mia is responsible." He cracked his gum. "In police work, assumptions can be lethal."

"If the police had done their job, and found Todd, this conversation—and my assumptions—wouldn't be happening."

Chuck leaned back in his creaky chair. He didn't know where this case was going, or how it was connected to Mia's son, but his cop instincts were buzzing a warning that something wasn't right. "I heard you have power of attorney for Mia. You're gonna be like her legal guardian, make the decisions for her while she's supposedly not capable of making them herself."

Karl raised one eyebrow. "Supposedly? My nephew's wife has tried to kill herself three times, and has most likely murdered her own son."

"She's *alleged* to have tried to kill herself three times and murdered her son."

"Semantics, Deputy Campbell. Semantics."

"So this power-of-attorney thing. It puts you in charge of her estate, right? Gives you access to a lot of money."

Karl's frown morphed into a menacing scowl. "What are you implying?"

Chuck shrugged innocently. "People kill each other all the time for the change in each other's pockets. Mia is worth several million. Several tens of millions, in fact, if I got my decimal places and commas right."

Karl Serrat lurched angrily to his feet. "I came here to file a missing person's report on my sister, not to be accused and interrogated."

Chuck met his furious stare steadily, trying to read the truth behind the furor. Honestly, he was having a hard time working up any sympathy for the man who'd fired his best friend in a hallway, in front of Chuck, Mia and a handful of deputies and hospital staff. In a small town like Eternal, gossip traveled fast. He'd bet Ty hadn't even been out the front door before phones all over town had been ringing with the news.

But none of that was an excuse for unprofessional

behavior, nor did it alleviate his obligation to investigate Nana Serrat's disappearance to the fullest.

Chuck picked up the missing person's report. "I'll see that this is passed on to the detectives."

Karl nodded curtly, turned on his heel and marched away. When he was gone, Chuck tagged the report urgent, added a yellow sticky note to the front asking the detective assigned to the case to call him, and sent it to dispatch for processing.

Back at his desk he pondered the mess his friend had gotten himself into. Chuck never would have thought Ty was the type to throw away everything he cared about for a woman—and a patient at that. Just went to show that no man was immune from the occasional propensity to think with his—with parts of his anatomy other than his brain.

Still, must be a hell of a woman to pull a stand-up guy like Ty so far over the edge so fast.

His curiosity piqued, he went to the evidence room and signed out the box of odds and ends belonging to Mia seized when the search warrant was executed on her house just before she'd been arrested. He'd seen something then he meant to follow up on and hadn't had time yet—

There it was, a fat yellow book with well-worn pages and a pretty waterfront landscape on the cover. Her journal.

He sat down and squirmed once before beginning to read. It wasn't comfortable, even for a cop, to pry into another person's most private possession—her diary. He wasn't sure he wanted to know the intimate details of Mia's life, especially given her state of mind over the last few years. But he figured he owed it to Ty, and to the kid, Todd, wherever he was, to turn over every stone in this investigation. Or in this case to turn every page.

He started on page one—when she'd still been in the hospital in California. The journal was an assignment from her doctors, he learned, to be her own record of how she felt day-to-day and a way to see her progress over the coming weeks and months.

The first entries were dark, filled with grief over the death of her husband, shame over what she'd done to herself, guilt for abandoning Todd. But over time, Chuck began to see glimpses of what he guessed Ty had seen. It was like her mental muscles were healing. He began to feel the strength in her words, the resilience. Months later, there were moments of pain, but there were also days and weeks of intense joy. A true gratefulness at being alive, having her son at her side. Her son. Most of the entries over the last two months dealt with Todd. Her pride in him. A little worry about him. Her love for him.

Didn't sound like a mother who would hurt her son, but then, he was no psychiatrist.

He reached an entry dated a month ago, and pulled the now-tasteless gum out of his mouth.

Now that was interesting. He'd almost missed it. It was a small addition at the bottom of a page, but it's magnitude was huge.

Standing, he settled his flat-brimmed hat on his head and checked his watch before he started out toward his patrol car. It was getting late, but that was too bad. He had a few more questions for the Serrat family.

Mia sat cross-legged on the floor of her unfurnished room. No cute little quarters with a rocking chair for her this time. No, this time she was in the max security. All she had was a thin little sleeping pad on the floor and a camera in the corner watching her every move.

She peered at the three little pills in her white paper cup, then up at the nurse who had handed them to her.

White. White shoes, white hose, white dress. Why did they have to wear all white? It wasn't very practical really. Too hard to keep clean. They must go through gallons of bleach. Probably just lined everyone up each night after their shifts and hosed them down with it from a pumper truck.

She laughed at the image and realized it wasn't funny. It was the drugs.

She shook her head trying to clear her mind. The drugs they'd given her at the police station still hadn't worn off, and here they were with more.

"If you don't take them, we'll have to give the medication by injection, and that's no fun."

No, she'd been down that route before. It wasn't fun at all.

Given no choice, she downed the pills, then raised her chin, opened her mouth wide and lifted her tongue for the nurse to see that she'd swallowed them without waiting to be asked. She knew the drill.

The nurse left, but to Mia's surprise, her exit wasn't followed by the loud click of the lock. Mia curled up on her side on the little mattress and let her thoughts swim in the pharmaceutical cocktail she'd been given.

She saw colors, so pretty, shifting like the ever-changing patterns inside a kaleidoscope. Eventually she saw pictures in the patterns. She saw Sam and she saw Todd, and she cried over them both.

Todd's mouth began to move, grinning wide and red like a circus clown's painted lips. He reached out to her, called her to sled down the hill with him one more time. He begged, he pleaded, and she could deny him nothing when he was smiling, happy. Her heart bloomed to see him so happy.

But as they zoomed down the slope, the painted lips began to drip. The red coloring ran down his chin like blood. A pear-shaped teardrop the size of a nickel appeared beneath one of his eyes, also painted in red, and scrolled down his cheek leaving a trail of crimson. Todd began to cry for real, and then to scream. He wouldn't stop screaming. She begged him to stop. She tried to hold him tight, but he seemed to disappear in her arms and all she was left holding was his coat.

His bloody coat.

Mia awoke with a start. The drugs muddling her mind made her slow to comprehend that she was not outside. She was in the hospital. There was no sledding hill. No coat.

There was also no Todd.

Moaning, she curled herself into the smallest ball she could and rocked herself, her arms locked around her legs.

What had she done? What had she done?

Nothing. She would never hurt her son.

Would she?

She couldn't be sure. She couldn't think. Her mind jumped from the school pageant, with Todd yelling that he hated her, to the sledding hill, to Ty, holding her, loving her, telling her everything would be all right.

He'd lied. Everything was not going to be all right.

Chapter 17

Ty sat on his couch in his darkened living room, his feet on the coffee table next to a bottle of beer that had gone warm hours ago, open but untouched. It hadn't been dark when he'd sat down. Sunshine had streamed through the windows. He realized that must have been hours ago—had he really been sitting here that long?

He was too tired to get up and turn the lights on. Too depressed to get up and go to bed.

He picked another textbook up off the floor and chucked it into the fireplace. Tomorrow he'd actually build a fire. Burn them all.

Christ, he was getting morose.

He forced himself to get up before he went comatose. Walked to the kitchen and got a bottle of water from the refrigerator and twisted off the cap.

A few moments later it sat abandoned, also untouched, next to the beer.

He'd screwed up big-time. Made a mistake—a misdiagnosis—that might have cost a little boy his life. Could have cost Mia her life, too, if Nana had been just a few minutes later getting home and finding her locked in the garage.

He'd let his personal feelings cloud his judgment. He'd wanted Mia to be well, so he'd seen her as well.

It didn't matter that the Kaiser had fired him; he didn't deserve to be a doctor.

The thing was…he still saw her as well. Even as he'd accused her, as he'd berated her and begged her to tell him where Todd was, he'd seen the strength in her eyes. The conviction.

The eyes could be deceiving.

Maybe he was grasping at straws because he just didn't want her to be guilty, but his mind wouldn't stop playing scenarios. Who would want to hurt her? Who would want Todd out of the way? It all came back to one thing every time: money.

Chuck had told him it looked like Karl would be granted power of attorney. That made him the most likely suspect. Could he have orchestrated all this? The attempts on Mia's life and Todd's disappearance?

It was possible, if not probable. Hell, not even remotely plausible. A one-in-a-million chance.

But it *was* possible.

And now Mia was in the Kaiser's hospital, all alone. No one on her side. No one to believe her. Believe *in* her.

Ty picked up his coat, cell phone and keys on his way to the door. He stopped at the threshold and dialed Chuck, one last sanity check. Hell, call it an intervention. If anyone could make him see the insanity of going back into the lion's den, Chuck could, but the call rolled to voice mail.

He stepped into the hall and latched the deadbolt on the door behind him.

One in a million was one too many for his peace of mind. If he was honest with himself, he'd admit he also just wanted to see her again. Even if it was on a four-by-four-inch black-and-white security screen.

Despite his attempts at stealth, the floor nurse caught him skulking down the second-floor hallway toward his office.

"What are you doing here?" Renee asked. "I heard you were…you know." She shrugged sympathetically.

"Yeah, I know." So did the rest of the hospital staff, obviously. The rumor mill must have been in high gear today.

"What will you do now?" she asked.

"I flip a mean burger."

"Flipping burgers isn't going to get you too far in paying back your student loans."

He really didn't want to think about that just yet. "I'll get by. I always do."

She shifted uncomfortably, then went with an easier topic. "What are you doing here?"

"Just came to pick up some things from my office." The lie flowed off his tongue too easily. "Personal stuff."

She looked at her watch. "At this time of night?"

"Thought I'd get it done when he wasn't likely to be around." No need to explain who *he* was.

"I don't think he's going to be happy about this, whether he's here or not." She looked uncertain. "How did you get in?"

"They haven't shut off my key-card access yet." He hoped that meant they hadn't revoked his computer IDs, either. "What's the harm? I don't want some stranger pawing through my stuff." He gave her his best charming grin. "What's the matter? Don't trust me?"

She gave in. "All right. Try to make it quick though, huh, before anyone else sees you."

"Will do."

He whistled lightly as he shuffled into his office trying to appear as if he hadn't a care in the world, then closed his door and slumped into his chair.

Sure enough, his computer codes were still good. He quickly hacked into the security network and brought up the Web cam shots. All the rooms in max security had cameras in the light fixtures. Patients on suicide watch were kept under twenty-four-hour surveillance from the nurses' station.

He found the video stream coming from her room,

saw her huddled in sleep on her pad. Unbidden, his finger lifted to touch the image of her face. The screen was cold, lifeless, so unlike her, and yet it was a long, long time before he could make himself pull his hand away.

Mia came awake slowly this time, gradually becoming aware that she wasn't alone. "Todd?"

She'd been dreaming about her son again. Thankfully this time there had been no blood.

"Todd?" she called again, more desperately.

"No, Mia, it's Citria."

Finally she pried her eyes open far enough to make out her sister-in-law's blurry features. Citria's head floated above her, seemingly disconnected from her body.

It was the drugs, had to be. She still couldn't see straight.

Mia's head rolled forward and back on her shoulders. Belatedly, she realized she'd drifted off again and Citria was shaking her.

"Mia, you've got to wake up. I've got to get you out of here."

"Out?" Mia managed a little bit more focus. "Why are you wearing that uniform?"

"I had to dress like a nurse to sneak in here. Luckily I know where Uncle Karl keeps his keys."

"I don't understand." Citria slung Mia's arm over her shoulder and hefted her up. Mia felt as if all of her muscles had been replaced by Jell-O. She tried to walk at Citria's urging, but couldn't take a step without help. "Where are we going?"

"Away from here." Citria half dragged, half carried her toward the door. "You're in danger here, Mia. I'm taking you somewhere safe."

"Danger." Mia frantically tried to make sense of what she was hearing. She wanted to leave, wanted it more than anything in the world except to have Todd back, although having Ty believe her rated up there pretty high, too, but there was a reason she couldn't go. What was it? *Oh.* "Can't leave. Under arrest."

She resisted Citria's attempts to drag her forward.

"Come on, Mia, we have to go."

"Can't."

"Mia, Todd is waiting for you."

That blew some of the cobwebs out of Mia's brain. "Todd?"

"I found him, Mia. It was Nana. She had him all along."

"Nana? Why?"

"She knew you were going to take him away from her, move back to California. She didn't want to lose him, and she didn't want you to have him. She always blamed you for Sam's death, you know."

"Blamed…me?"

"He moved to California because that's where you lived. If he'd stayed here, he would never have been in that accident. But we don't have time to talk about this now. I have to get you out of here. It's not safe here. Uncle Karl is in on it, too. He just wants your money. I have to get you somewhere he can't find you. I have to get you back to Todd."

Mia nodded drunkenly, almost afraid to hope that it was true. That her son was safe, that she was going to be with him soon. "Todd…"

Digging deep, she found the strength in her legs and the will to stumble out of the little locked room with Citria.

The pain in Ty's back roused him from a fitful sleep. Damn cheap chair. The antique swivel desk chair was hell on his posture. Of course, sleeping with his head laid on his folded arms over the desk wasn't much good for his spine, either.

Oh well, he wouldn't have to worry about the old chair anymore. He didn't work here any longer.

Remembering why he *was* here, he lifted his head and rubbed the back of his hand across his eyes. The computer monitor slowly came into focus. Only, instead of seeing Mia's room, all he saw was a gray screen. He turned up the brightness button on the monitor. Tapped a few commands on the keyboard.

Nothing.

A pit of dread spread in his belly. In the year he'd worked here, he'd never seen the security equipment fail like this. He had a bad feeling…

All vestiges of sleep were gone in a heady rush of adrenaline, his long strides ate the distance to Mia's room in seconds. A quick look through the window confirmed his worst fear.

Mia was gone.

Inside, he reached up to the lens of the security camera, and dread turned to fear.

Oh God, she'd been telling the truth all along.

The night nurse, Renee, hurried into the room. "What are you doing here—"

"Mia's gone, call the cops." He was already on his way down the hall toward the side door. They had to have gone out the side. The other direction would have taken them directly by Renee's desk.

"She escaped?"

"No," he called back. "The lens on the security camera has been spray-painted. Someone took her."

Ty wound through the hospital corridors, mentally ticking off the seconds in his head. Seconds Mia was in danger. Seconds he was losing trying to find her.

Finally he reached the side door. Exterior doors in this section were alarmed. A key was necessary to open them without setting off a racket designed to draw a lot of attention very quickly. Yet the halls were silent.

Either they hadn't gone out this way or…her abductor had a key.

Karl?

It didn't seem possible, but Karl would know about the cameras, and how best to disable them. He would certainly have keys.

Crap.

He slammed the door open. The alarm whooped and chattered, announcing to the world that he was coming. So much for sneaking up on anybody.

The silvery light of a half moon glimmered off the snow outside. Ty's breath puffed in front of him in the cold night air. He didn't see anyone and was stymied on where to go next when he looked down. Footprints!

He followed the trail to the northeast corner of the building. The wind was blowing, and his cheeks stung in the cold. But his blood ran hot in his veins.

One set of footprints was clear. The other distorted, as if someone was being half dragged, half pulled.

Mia. She'd been pretty heavily sedated, he'd bet. She might not even understand what was happening to her, that she was in danger.

A taillight flashed from the little alcove where the Dumpsters sat. Ty pasted his back to the side of the building and tiptoed toward it. Someone had shut off the alarm and he could hear the engine now, puttering softly. He looked around for a weapon—a board or a pipe or a brick—but found nothing.

Resolutely, he crept forward and peeked around the corner.

What the hell?

It was a sheriff's office car. He'd told Renee to call the cops, but they couldn't have gotten here already. Besides, the light bar on top of the car was dark and silent. Deadly silent.

He squinted, and in the backseat could just make out a slumped form.

Mia!

As he lifted his foot to step forward, pain exploded

in the back of his skull. The silvery light of the moon wavered, then winked out, and Ty fell face-first unconscious into the snow.

Chapter 18

Mia tried to focus on the blurry shape outside the car without success. "Citria?"

No answer.

Whoever it was seemed to be dragging or carrying something heavy.

Todd? Her heart accelerated. What was wrong with him?

She scooted across the seat when the car door opened. Citria leaned in, pushing and grunting, thrusting something—someone—into her arms.

Not Todd. Too big.

She willed her drugged eyes to focus. It was Ty.

She turned back to Citria. "Wh-what's happening?"

He was warm and his chest rose and fell slowly with each soughed breath, but he wouldn't wake up when she shook him. She felt something warm and sticky where his head lay on her thigh. Blood. "What happened to Ty? What's wrong with him?"

Nothing about this made sense. Citria climbed in the front of the car and put it in gear.

"Where are we going?" The sense that something was terribly wrong blew a few of the cobwebs out of her head. She was in a police car. The backseat. A steel barrier separated her from her sister-in-law in front. Why was Citria driving a police car?

"I told you. I'm taking you to Todd."

"Where? Where is he?"

"The old riding stable. That's where Nana's been hiding him."

Mia remembered the old stable. Sam had told her many times about the jumping lessons he'd taken there. The shows he'd competed in and the ribbons he'd won. One of her favorite pictures in her house in California was of a teenage Sam, grin spread ear to ear, on a gleaming black horse sailing over a brush wall as if on the wings of angels.

She'd taken Todd to the stables a couple of months ago and been sad to see the weathered sign out front faded and hanging lopsided on one chain, the rusted gate locked shut. It had gone out of business long ago—just one more piece of Sam she'd lost.

Ty moaned in her lap. She felt the wound on the back of his head and pressed the hem of her shirt against the crease to stanch the flow of blood. His eyelids fluttered and his lips moved soundlessly, but consciousness still eluded him.

Mia wished he would wake up. She wished he would help her sort out what was happening.

"Why are you taking me?" Mia asked. "Where are the police?"

"Just shut up with the questions already, would you?" The eyes that met Mia's in the rearview mirror gleamed darkly. Insanely. "It'll all be over soon."

Ty first became aware of the world beyond the pounding in his head when a blast of cold air slapped him in the face. He opened his eyes to find himself lying across the backseat of a police car. Squinting, he could make out Mia's worried features leaning over him.

And her sister-in-law holding a gun on them through the open car door.

"W'as going on?" he slurred. His tongue didn't quite seem connected to his brain. He tried to sit but gave up when a fresh round of explosions rocked his skull.

Mia answered, never taking her eyes off Citria's gun. "I don't know."

"Get out, both of you." Citria waved the barrel of the gun toward the barn door a few feet away.

Ty wasn't sure who was less coordinated as they scrambled out of the car and onto their feet, him or Mia. She wobbled, and he caught her elbow. He stumbled and she held his shirt. At least she didn't seem to be hurt. Still feeling the effects of the sedatives, he guessed.

"What is this place?" he asked Mia.

"She says Todd is here. She says Nana took him."

Ty frowned, trying to think between drumbeats in his head. If Nana took Todd, how come Citria was the one holding the gun on them?

The old barn door creaked as Citria pushed it and it lumbered aside on its rails. She motioned Mia and Ty inside. The scents of musty hay, stale oats and manure still permeated the barn.

"Todd?" Mia called, looking around hopefully.

"It's no use. He's locked up tight and sound asleep in the tack room. He won't be waking up anytime soon. I made sure of that."

Ty could guess how she did that. Damn, he hoped she knew how to dose drugs for a child. Otherwise, Todd could be comatose or worse. "What did you give him?"

Citria threw him a snooty look that said she didn't deign to answer. She pushed him toward an open stall down the barn's center aisle.

Inside, Nana Serrat sat on the dirt floor, her wrists and ankles bound. Her eyes were wide and filled with terror above the duct tape that covered her mouth.

"Damn it," Ty said, outrage bringing the strength back to his limbs. He strode across the stall and eased the tape off Nana's mouth. Tears rolled down her cheeks as she thanked him silently with her look. Mia knelt beside them and started unwinding the tape from her wrists.

"Leave her," Citria said, and cocked the hammer on the revolver.

"Sweetheart," Nana said, the use of the endearment sounding out of place. "Why are you doing this?"

"You know why, Mom." She circled the three-some crouched on the floor, keeping the gun leveled in their direction. "I've waited for years for it to be my turn. For *me* to matter."

Nana's brow wrinkled. "I don't understand."

"Nearly all my life it was all about Sam. He was the one who mattered. He was the golden boy who got good grades. He was the captain of the soccer team. He started his own business and made millions." She bit her lip. "I was the one who flunked out of nursing school."

"Darling, I loved you both. I've always loved you bo—"

"And you." She swung the gun toward Mia. Ty instinctively pulled her closer to him. "You had the perfect life, living in a big mansion in California. You had the perfect husband, the perfect child. You had everything I wanted."

"You were married once," Mia said quietly.

Citria sniffed. "For a year and a half. And during that time I had two miscarriages. Then the jerk dumped me."

Ty wished he'd known all this sooner. He might have put the pieces together. Sibling rivalry becomes a persecution syndrome. Multiple miscarriages create a feeling of inadequacy. He should have dug deeper. He should have believed Mia. Believed there was another answer.

"Then Sam was killed in that accident, and a few months later you went nuts and I thought finally… *finally* it was going to be my turn. Then Todd came to live with us, and at first I thought it was going to be like having Sam around to take the limelight all over again, but he was just a little boy, and he was hurting, and I did my best—I really did—to help him. To be a mother to him."

"He has a mother, Citria," Mia said.

Citria's hands shook on the handle of the revolver. "No. No. You don't deserve him."

Mia opened her mouth, a protest on her lips, Ty was sure. He squeezed her arm, hoping she understood to back off, slow down. Not to press too hard. Citria was on the verge of going completely off the deep end, and since she was the one holding the gun, he'd rather not be here when that happened.

Mia closed her mouth and took a deep breath before she opened it again. Message received, Ty thought.

"Maybe I don't, Citria," she said. "But this is not the way. What are you going to do? Kill us all?"

Citria grinned wickedly. "No, you are. At least that's what the cops will think. Your lover here sprung you from the loony bin. You brought him here, where you'd stashed Todd, but Nana figured it out. She found you somehow. Everything went horribly wrong and you killed them all, then popped yourself. It'll be a textbook murder-suicide. Case closed."

"Please, Citria, don't," Nana begged. "Don't do this."

"Oh, don't worry, Grandma Nana. The precious golden boy will be fine. I am sorry about you, though. I hadn't planned to include you in this, but once you found me here with Todd, I really had no choice, did I? Besides, it will be better this way. Uncle Karl may have control of Todd's inheritance, but Nana here is no pauper, either. And *I* am the beneficiary in *her* will." She cocked her head and laughed, a crazy twitter like a tiny bird with a worm. "Maybe we'll move to France, just the two of us. I'll raise him like my own, I promise." She aimed the promise at Mia.

"Citria," Ty jumped in. "You need to take a step back. Think about how you'll look back on this in a few—"

"Oh, please. Don't try the therapy routine, Dr. Hansen. I've had enough of that from Uncle Karl over the years."

"Okay, then think about this. You're going to spend the rest of your life in jail if you kill any of us. Your story is full of holes. It won't take the cops ten minutes to figure out what really happened. And then your life is over."

Her eyes narrowed. "What holes?"

"Like the fact that the only car here is a police car. How did Mia and I supposedly get here? How did Nana get here? And where is Chuck, by the way?"

Ty didn't like the fact there was no sign of the deputy here.

"The cop?" Citria asked nonchalantly. "Oh, he's in the trunk."

Citria giggled again. God, Ty wanted to ask if his friend was alive or dead, but he wasn't sure he really wanted to know yet. If Chuck was dead, then it might be too late to save any of them. Citria had already committed a death penalty offense. There was no turning back for her now.

He preferred to think he still had a chance. That they all still had a chance.

"Don't worry your pretty little head about holes," Citria suggested, then shrugged. "Except the ones you're going to be sporting in a few minutes. Nana's car is still parked in the outbuilding behind the barn, and as for you two…I guess you hitchhiked."

"What about the deputy?"

"He's going to have a terrible accident tonight. His car is going right off the bridge and into the river. These snowy roads get *so* slippery. It's dangerous out there."

Ty let out the breath he'd been holding. So Chuck was still alive. For now.

"Enough," Citria said. "It's been a long night, and I still have to take care of the deputy and get to a pay phone to make the 911 call saying someone heard shots over by the old stable. I want this over with as soon as possible. Who's first?" The gun swung from Nana to Mia to Ty and back. "Sorry, Mom."

"No!" Ty lurched across Mia toward her mother-in-law as the gun's retort cracked in his ears. The breath whooshed out of him when he hit the ground. At first he thought the breath had just been knocked out of him. It wasn't until he rolled over and saw the bloom of red across the side of his ribs that he realized he'd been hit.

The pain caught up with him a half second later.

Mia screamed and scrambled toward him. "Ty!"

The barrel of the gun tracked her movement. Citria's finger tightened on the trigger and he yanked Mia toward him. Down.

Another figure flew through the doorway into the horse stall, knocking Citria down. The gun slid aside and Karl Serrat grabbed it, slid it into the waistband of his pants and then straddled Citria, holding her wrists down while she bucked and fought him with all her might. She tried to bite him, and he flipped her over, crossing her arms over her chest in a strait-jacket hold.

Sirens blared in the distance.

"Mia, get the duct tape. It's right outside the door."

Karl's order was like a wake-up call to both Ty and Mia. He loosened his grip on her, finally realizing they were both still alive, and she crawled across the floor to the aisle.

Citria looked dazedly up at her uncle, her body suddenly going slack. "It's okay, Uncle Karl. I'm going now."

Mia had reached his side with the tape.

"Going where?" Karl asked, frowning. Gently he turned his limp niece to bring her hands around front. With one quick motion, she jerked her right hand free. Mia realized what she was doing before anyone else and grabbed for Citria's hand, but missed.

Citria pulled the gun from Karl's waistband and placed the barrel under her chin. "To France," she said dreamily, and pulled the trigger.

Chapter 19

Ty was resting comfortably in his bed at the Eternal Emergency Care Clinic when the Kaiser walked in—as comfortably as a man can when he has a concussion and two cracked ribs. At least the bullet that grazed his side hadn't punctured his lung.

He tried to sit up straighter as Karl Serrat approached.

"Don't," the Kaiser waved. "Don't."

Ty slumped against his pillow.

"How are you?" Karl asked.

"I'm fine," he lied. "How's Nana?" He wasn't ready for the harder questions yet.

"She's…sad."

"And you?"

"I'm sad, too, I guess."

He ducked his chin to his chest. He couldn't hold back any longer. "What about Mia?" He hadn't heard anything about her since he'd been admitted.

"She's gone, son," the Kaiser said, his voice uncharacteristically kind.

"Gone? Gone, as in—"

Karl dismissed his panic with a wave. "Gone as in back to California. She booked a flight for herself and Todd as soon as the police were done with her."

Ty frowned. "You let her go?"

"I don't think I could have stopped her." He smiled briefly. "She'll be okay, though. She's a strong girl."

"Yeah, that she is."

After a moment of uncomfortable silence, Ty asked, "How did you find us?" Between the surgery and sedation, he hadn't caught up on the full story.

"Your friend Deputy Campbell is the one who figured out Citria was behind Todd's disappearance."

"Chuck?"

Karl nodded. "He'd found a few entries in Mia's diary. She wrote that she was concerned about Citria, that she saw some of the signs of depression that she'd seen in herself two years ago. She tried to get Citria to get help, but said Citria was jealous of her, and of Sam and Todd. She said Citria was paranoid, and had accused her of trying to get rid of her so she could be Nana's only family. Mia was really worried about Citria. She had decided to talk to Nana, and to

me, about her just before this whole mess started
with the fall from Shilling's Bluff."

"She's good."

"Mmm, yes. Maybe she should consider going
into psychiatry."

Ty smiled at that. He doubted Mia wanted to be
within spitting distance of a mental-health facility
ever again.

"The deputy woke me up to talk to me about
Citria. I realized his theory could be correct, but I
didn't know where to find her. I couldn't sleep after
the deputy left, so eventually I went back to the
hospital and pulled some old records from when
Citria was treated for depression during her teenage
years. She mentioned the riding stable a lot. It was
her safe place. So I got in the car and drove."

"And called the cops, I assume, since the cavalry
arrived right after you did."

"Yes."

It was amazing they had all survived. Todd had
slept like a babe through the whole ordeal, and
snored softly against his mother's chest after being
freed from the locked tack room. Chuck had been
freed from the trunk of his patrol car with only minor
injury to his pride and a little frostbite. It seemed
Citria had gotten the drop on him when he went to
question her, much as she'd gotten the drop on Ty at
the hospital, and stolen his car and his gun.

The uncomfortable silence stretched between them
again. Karl finally broke it. "I owe you an apology, son."

Ty pressed his lips together and shook his head. "I was way out of line with Mia."

Karl smiled. "That's a debate for another day. But that's not what I'm apologizing for."

Ty raised his gaze and his eyebrows.

"I've been riding you hard ever since you got here. I didn't recognize your name on the residency application. It wasn't until I saw you—" he nodded down at the scars on Ty's bare arm "—and saw those that it clicked."

"Clicked?"

Karl stood and put his hands in his pockets, paced to the window. "I knew your mother years ago. She was a patient of mine when I first started at MHMH."

"You treated her?"

"I thought I did. I was young and arrogant. I thought I could cure the world with a good couch and a few months of therapy. I patted her on the head and prescribed some meds and sent her home."

Karl turned and looked at Ty. "To you."

Sonofabitch.

"It wasn't until years later that I found out what she'd done to you—been doing to you. You were in high school I think when a teacher finally realized what was happening and Child Services pulled you out of the home."

"Ninth grade."

"I made a mistake. A big one, and you suffered for it. I'm sorry."

Ty cleared his throat. His thoughts whirled. Anger

flew by, but cleared out quickly. He was too tired, too hurt to be angry. "It happens. We're doctors, not gods. None of us are all-knowing."

"Maybe you should keep that in mind when you look back on what happened with Mia."

"There's a big difference between making a medical mistake and having a…relationship with a patient."

"I'm going to forget you said that."

"Because it's a breach of medical ethics?"

Karl guffawed. An honest laugh. "Because you're talking about my niece, and there are some things an uncle just should not know."

He sat down next to the bed again. "I should leave you. You need your rest. But before I go, I have something for you." He pulled an envelope from the inside pocket of his suit coat.

Ty turned it over in his hands. "What is it?"

"A plane ticket to California, and a letter of recommendation to one of the best mental-health facilities on the West Coast. The director there is an old alum chum. He said he'd be happy to have you on board."

Ty frowned.

"Of course, you'd be welcome to come back to work at MHMH, but I didn't think—"

Ty shook his head. He turned the envelope over again. "California?"

Karl Serrat feigned innocence poorly. "Did I mention that Mia is in California?"

Christmas morning, Mia bit her lip and watched silently as her baffled son opened up the last of his presents. A red rope with a clip on one end and a handle on the other. A ceramic bowl with hearts and paw prints around the rim. A large plaid pillow.

Reaching for the last gift, he looked up at her in puzzlement. "Mo-om?"

"Just open it."

He sighed and tore at the red foil wrapping over the odd-shaped present. When he got his first look at it, his eyes widened. He blinked as if he couldn't believe it. He was holding a bone-shaped picture frame with a picture of a cute yellow dog behind the glass and a sticky note that said, "Go to the utility room to find your last present."

"Mo-om?" His little fingers tightened on the frame. "MOM!" He jumped up and ran for the stairs.

Just before Mia had left Eternal, she'd gone to say goodbye to Nana one last time. Before she left, Nana shared Todd's confession about the Christmas gift he wanted but was afraid to ask for: a dog.

Three days ago she'd visited the Humane Society shelter and adopted an adorable ten-week-old golden retriever mix. It had been murder keeping the secret from Todd until this morning.

It was worth it though, judging by the high-pitched barks and little-boy squeals of delight coming from downstairs.

She picked up the leash and went to watch. The pair was spinning wildly around the utility room. Mia wasn't sure who was more excited, dog or boy, but one thing she was sure of—they were both an accident looking for a place to happen.

"All right, all right. How about we take the new family member out for a walk on the beach and work off some of that energy?"

Todd had leash and pup in hand and was making his way down the stone staircase to the waterfront before Mia could turn around.

The beach was nearly deserted—it was still Christmas morning, after all. She and Todd and the pup walked and skipped and waded ankle-deep in the surf. They sang carols and threw sticks to be fetched and held hands.

Mia was thankful for every second of it. She'd come so close to losing him, but he'd come through the ordeal relatively unscathed. He didn't understand all that had happened—Citria had kept him well sedated most of the time. Mia had him seeing a therapist again, just to be sure. And she made certain to reassure him of her love every chance she got.

Her own mental wounds were healing, as well. Todd was alive and happy and they were together— that was all that mattered. Her life was complete. Or so she told herself. She didn't let herself examine the one empty place left in her heart too closely.

Todd laughed at the pup's antics, and she smiled. "What are you going to name him?"

She was talking to Todd, but looking down the beach, to where someone was walking down the sand, feet bare and ankle-deep in water as she and Todd had been, his hands shoved in the pockets of his jeans. His head was down and he looked deep in thought.

He also looked familiar.

Her breath caught. "Ty?"

She hurried down the sand. Todd was off in the other direction playing with the puppy, thankfully.

"Mia." It was a sigh and a surrender. He wrapped his arms around her and pulled her close, buried his rough jaw against her neck.

They stood that way a long while. Finally he let her go and stepped back, grinning down at her with a shy smile. It was a look she hadn't seen on him before.

"You're okay?" she asked. "You're out of the hospital."

He held his hands out to the sides as if for inspection. "Good as new."

She wrinkled her nose. "I knew that, actually. I've been calling the hospital every day. I wouldn't even have left Eternal if your doctor hadn't assured me you were going to be okay."

"I know."

Mia looked around to check on Ty. He was playing down the beach, at a safe distance from the water, suspiciously oblivious to the reunion going on nearby. She frowned.

Ty fessed up. "I caught him yesterday when he was playing out in the yard. Paid him ten bucks to give us a few minutes when I finally got up the nerve to talk to you."

She shook her head, screwed up her face. "Got

up the nerve? And he took ten dollars from you to ignore us?"

"Worth every penny, though I only offered him five at first. Guy's gonna be a killer businessman, just like his father."

They both laughed. Mia would have to talk to Ty about taking advantage of friends, though. Another day.

Ty pulled his shoulders back. The humor fell from his face. "I wanted to make sure I had time to apologize properly."

"Apologize?"

He cleared his throat. "For not believing in you."

Her heart thudded dully in her chest. Of all her unseen wounds, that one was the deepest. Deep, but not mortal.

"I let my past color my judgment. I made a mistake. A big one."

Mia looked deep into his hazel eyes, gauged the depth of his wounds, and decided they were, quite possibly, much more serious than her own. But what to do about it? Morosity wasn't going to heal either of them.

She quirked up one corner of her mouth and put her hands on her hips. "Well, then I guess we can't ever have any kind of relationship."

His face pinched.

"I mean, I am, after all, perfect. And I expect everyone around me to be perfect, too."

His frown turned to puzzlement.

She lightened her tone even further, put on a frothy

air to make her point. "I mean, I've never let my emotions get the better of me like that. I've never lost sight of what was important, of the truth, because I couldn't see past my own pain."

Enlightenment dawned on his handsome face. "Don't make fun of me."

"I would never make fun of you," she said earnestly, then stepped up close and poked him in the belly. "But I might make fun of us."

"You might, huh?"

"I might. So are you going to kiss me, or what?"

He grinned. Their lips were nearly touching already. "I'm thinking about it."

"Here's a tip from one imperfect human to another," she whispered. "Don't think so much."

Their bodies came together as if they'd never been apart. It was a reunion of heart, spirit and soul. They stayed like that until Mia looked over Ty's shoulder and saw Todd watching curiously. And pacing, the puppy at his heels.

"I think someone thinks his time is up," she said.

"Ten bucks only buys so much."

Holding hands, they turned and walked toward Todd together.

Ty looked up at the mansion on the hilltop. "So, this is the old homestead."

Mia winced. "I've been thinking about downsizing."

"I don't know." He looked at the rocky hillside, green ferns and yellow and blue wildflowers popping from every crevice, the purple bougainvillea draped over the wrought-iron fence at the top, the clear blue skies, the turquoise surf. "I could get used to the view."

She stopped, held him back. "Does that mean you're staying?"

"Maybe. If you wouldn't mind having me around."

She grinned. "I wouldn't mind."

"Then I'm staying."

Todd let out a war whoop and wrapped his little arms around them both while the puppy bounced and barked at his feet.

Mia framed his face with her palms. The sun glowed off her face and her eyes shone with life.

"Good thing," she said. "Otherwise I'd have to go all the way back to Massachusetts just to drag you back here."

He laughed. God, he liked her moxie.

She cut off his laughter with a kiss, deep and powerful.

He liked her moxie very, very much.

* * * * *

*Fan favorite Leslie Kelly is bringing her
readers a fantasy so scandalous,
we're calling it FORBIDDEN!*

*Look for
PLAY WITH ME
Available February 2010 from
Harlequin® Blaze™.*

"AREN'T YOU GOING TO SAY 'Fly me' or at least 'Welcome aboard'?"

Amanda Bauer didn't. The softly muttered word that actually came out of her mouth was a lot less welcoming. And had fewer letters. Four, to be exact.

The man shook his head and tsked. "Not exactly the friendly skies. Haven't caught the spirit yet this morning?"

"Make one more airline-slogan crack and you'll be walking to Chicago," she said.

He nodded once, then pushed his sunglasses onto the top of his tousled hair. The move revealed blue eyes that matched the sky above. And yeah. They were twinkling. Damn it.

"Understood. Just, uh, promise me you'll say 'Coffee, tea or me' at least once, okay? Please?"

Amanda tried to glare, but that twinkle sucked the annoyance right out of her. She could only draw in a slow breath as he climbed into the plane. As she watched her passenger disappear into the small jet, she had to wonder about the trip she was about to take.

Coffee and tea they had, and he was welcome to them. But her? Well, she'd never even considered making a move on a customer before. Talk about unprofessional.

And yet...

Something inside her suddenly wanted to take a chance, to be a little outrageous.

How long since she had done indecent things—or decent ones, for that matter—with a sexy man? Not since before they'd thrown all their energies into expanding Clear-Blue Air, at the very least. She hadn't had time for a lunch date, much less the kind of lust-fest she'd enjoyed in her younger years. The kind that lasted for entire weekends and involved not leaving a bed except to grab the kind of sensuous food that could be smeared onto—and eaten off—someone else's hot, naked, sweat-tinged body.

She closed her eyes, her hand clenching tight on the railing. Her heart fluttered in her chest and she tried to make herself move. But she couldn't—not climbing up, but not backing away, either. Not physically, and not in her head.

Was she really considering this? God, she hadn't even looked at the stranger's left hand to make sure he was available. She had no idea if he was actually attracted to her or just an irrepressible flirt. Yet something inside was telling her to take a shot with this man.

It was crazy. Something she'd never considered.

Yet right now, at this moment, she was definitely considering it. If he was available…could she do it? Seduce a stranger. Have an anonymous fling, like something out of a blue movie on late-night cable?

She didn't know. All she knew was that the flight to Chicago was a short one so she had to decide quickly. And as she put her foot on the bottom step and began to climb up, Amanda suddenly had to wonder if she was about to embark on the ride of her life.

New Year, New Man!

For the perfect New Year's punch,
blend the following:

- *One woman determined to find her inner vixen*
- *A notorious—and notoriously hot!—playboy*
- *A provocative New Year's Eve bash*
- *An impulsive kiss that leads to a night of*
explosive passion!

When the clock hits midnight Claire Daniels
kisses the guy standing closest to her, but
the kiss doesn't end after the bells stop ringing….

Look for

Moonstruck

by *USA TODAY* bestselling author

JULIE KENNER

Available January

---

red-hot reads

www.eHarlequin.com

HARLEQUIN
Ambassadors

Want to share your passion for reading Harlequin® Books?

Become a Harlequin Ambassador!

Harlequin Ambassadors are a group of passionate and well-connected readers who are willing to share their joy of reading Harlequin® books with family and friends.

You'll be sent all the tools you need to spark great conversation, including free books!

All we ask is that you share the romance with your friends and family!

You'll also be invited to have a say in new book ideas and exchange opinions with women just like you!

To see if you qualify* to be a Harlequin Ambassador, please visit www.HarlequinAmbassadors.com.

*Please note that not everyone who applies to be a Harlequin Ambassador will qualify. For more information please visit www.HarlequinAmbassadors.com.

Thank you for your participation.

BAP09BPA

REQUEST YOUR FREE BOOKS!

2 FREE NOVELS
PLUS
2 FREE GIFTS!

Sparked by Danger, Fueled by Passion.

HARLEQUIN® HISTORICAL:
Where love is timeless

From chivalrous knights
to roguish rakes, look for the
variety Harlequin® Historical
has to offer every month.